SHAN FOLK LORE STORIES

FROM THE

HILL AND WATER COUNTRY

BY

WILLIAM C. GRIGGS, M. D.

WILDSIDE PRESS

www.wildsidepress.com

TO MY FRIEND

J. N. Cushing, D. D., F. R. A. S.

Principal of the American Baptist College, Rangoon, and Senior
Shan   Missionary,   the   greatest   authority   upon
Shan literature, and the translator of the
Bible   into   that   language,   this
little book is dedicated by

THE AUTHOR

INTRODUCTION

THE following stories have been taken from the great mass of unwritten lore that is to the black-eyed, brown-skinned boys and girls of the Shan mountain country of Burma what "Jack the Giant Killer" and "Cinderella" are to our own children.

The old saw as to the songs and laws of a country may or may not be true. I feel confident, however, that stories such as these, being as they are purely native, with as little admixture of Western ideas as it was possible to give them in dressing them in their garment of English words, will give a better insight into what the native of Burma really is, his modes of thought and ways of looking at and measuring things, than a treatise thrice as long and representing infinitely more literary merit than will be found in these little tales ; and at the same time I hope they will be found to the average reader, at least, more interesting.

It may, perhaps, be not out of place to say a little of the "hpeas" who appear so frequently in these stories. The hpea is the Burman nat, and is "a being superior to men and inferior to Brahmas, and having its dwelling in one of the six celestial regions" (Doctor Cushing's "Shan-English Dictionary"). They are universally worshiped by the inhabitants of Burma.

If a man has fever, the best thing to do is to "*ling hpea*," that is, to feed the spirits, and the sufferer therefore offers rice, betel-nut, painted sticks, etc. Some kinds of *hpeas* live in the sacred banyan trees, and frequently have I seen men, after a long day's march in the jungle, sit shivering on the ground when within an arm's length lay good dry fire-wood. It had fallen, however, from a tree in which lived a *hpea*, and not a man would dare touch it. Big combs of honey may be in the nests of the wild bees, but it is safe from the hungry traveler if it is sheltered by such a tree. Some watch over wells, tanks, and lakes, and it is notorious throughout the Southern Shan States, that a promising young American missionary, who was drowned while shooting, met his death by being dragged to the bottom of the lake by the guardian spirit, who had become incensed at him for killing a water-fowl on his domains.

In Shan folk-lore the hero does not "marry and live happy ever after," but he becomes the king of the country.

AMERICAN BAPTIST SHAN MISSION HOUSE,
BHAMO, BURMA, 1902.

CONTENTS

A LAUNG KHIT   9

HOW BOH HAN ME GOT HIS TITLE 19

THE TWO CHINAMEN 32

THE STORY OF THE PRINCESS NANG KAM UNG 45

HOW THE HARE DECEIVED THE TIGER 57

THE STORY OF THE TORTOISE 66

THE SPARROW'S WONDERFUL BROOD 78

HOW THE WORLD WAS CREATED 85

HOW THE KING OF PAGAN CAUGHT THE THIEF 92

LIST OF ILLUSTRATIONS

" Each year at the Feast of Lights . . . she prayed "....... *10*

" The man standing at the top of the tree was the long-lost brother "... *37*

" Again the cunning hare deceived the tiger ".................. *63*

" ' I am nothing but a tortoise swimming in the lake ' "...... *67*

" On his way he saw what seemed to be a bed of flowers "... *79*

FOLK LORE STORIES

"A LAUNG KHIT." [1]

ONCE upon a time there was a woman who lived in the State of Lai Hka. She was a very pious woman and always gave the best rice and *puc* to the priests as they walked, rice *chattie* in hand, through the city in the early morning. Every year when the girls and boys went to the river and filled their chatties with water to throw over the pagodas and idols to insure a good rainy season and abundant crops, she always had the largest bucket of the clearest water and threw it higher than anybody else. She carried the sweetest flowers to the *zayat* every evening, and on worship days took rice in the prettiest of cups made of banana leaves and offered to the Gautamas in the idol-house.

But she was not happy. When her neighbors went to the pagodas they had their little ones tied upon their backs or running at their sides, but she had no child whom she could take with her, none to whom she could tell stories of the great Lord Sa Kyah who rules over the spirits in the *hpea* country, and so she was sad. She was getting old too, and often envied the women

---

[1] "'A Laung,' one who is progressing toward a divine state; an incipient deity."—*Cushing's "Shan Dictionary," p. 586.*

who lived near who had bright boys to run errands and girls to help in the house. Each year at the Feast of Lights, when she sent her little candle floating down the river, she prayed for a child, but in vain.

At last she made a pilgrimage to a pagoda where folks said was a *parah* who would give anything that was asked of him. Bright and early she set out, and on her head as an offering she carried an image of a tiger and one of a man, and when she arrived at the pagoda she offered the images and prayed for a son.

While she was praying at the pagoda, Lord Sa Kyah heard her, took pity on her, and promised her a son. But, alas! when he was born, to his mother's great sorrow, instead of being the beautiful boy she hoped for he was nothing but a frog.

Lord Sa Kyah in order to comfort her, however, told her that her son was really a great *hpea*, and that after one year and seven months he would change into the most handsome man in all the hill and water country.

All the women scoffed and made fun of the poor mother, and all through the village she was called Myeh Khit, or "Frog's Mother," but she bore their jeers in silence and never reviled in return.

Now the king of the country had seven daughters. All were married except one, and one day Myeh Khit went to him to ask for this daughter in marriage for her son. The king was of course very angry that she should ask that his only remaining daughter should marry a frog, but he spoke deceitfully, called his daughter and asked her if she would be willing to ac-

" Each year at the Feast of Lights . . . she prayed."

Page 10.

cept a frog for a husband. Like a dutiful daughter
she told him that she would "follow his words" and
do as he wished, as she had no will apart from his.

The king then called the woman and said : "O
woman, I will give my only remaining daughter to your
son, but I make one stipulation. You must build a
road, paved and properly built, from the market-place
to my palace ; the sides must be decorated with painted
bamboos, and the work must be done within seven days
or you shall die. Now go, and prepare for the work,
and at the end of the seven days I will make ready the
marriage feast for my daughter or order the executioner
to take off your head."

In great distress Myeh Khit returned to her home
and sat down on the floor of her house and wept. All
day long she bewailed her hopeless condition. In vain
her son asked her the cause of her sorrow. Afraid of
grieving him she would not tell him ; but at last when
six out of the seven days had passed, and knowing the
fate that awaited her on the morrow, she told him how
she had gone to the king with her request, and the time
being almost expired, that she must make ready to die
on the morrow.

"The executioner's sword has already been sharp-
ened, my son," she said, "and to-day in bazaar they
were talking of it, and promising to meet one another
at the palace to-morrow when the sun should be overhead."

As a last resource she made ready food and sweet-
meats. She took paddy and placed it over the fire till

the heat broke the husks and the pure white grains appeared. These she mixed with the whitest of sugar, and as she was too poor to own plates, she went into the jungle to where the new bamboo was bursting through its green prison, and taking the broad coverings of the new leaves she fashioned them into dishes and offered them with many prayers for help to Lord Sa Kyah.

"Our lord knoweth that my son can do nothing," she cried. "He has not even hands to help, and what can our lord's slave do to avoid the great trouble to which I have arrived?"

That night in the lovely *hpea* country the mighty Lord Sa Kyah reclined on his golden throne of state. By and by the velvet mat became so hot that he could sit upon it no longer, and looking down he saw, squatting before him on the floor, a frog.

"O our lord," said the frog, "I come to remind our lord that he is his slave's father. My mother, our lord's slave, has arrived at great sorrow, and unless our lord pities us and takes compassion on our lord's slave, she will arrive at destruction to-morrow. Graciously do this act of kindness, O chief of all the *hpeas*."

Lord Sa Kyah took pity on his son and promised to help him. The four strongest spirits in his kingdom were four *hpeas*. They were twins and the name of the first two was Nan Ta Re and that of the second Hte Sa Kyung. These powerful spirits he ordered to complete the road during the night.

The next morning when the king arose he looked

forth from his palace and a most wonderful sight met
his gaze. He rubbed his eyes, for he believed they deceived him. He pinched himself to see whether he was
really awake or whether he was dreaming. For a wonderful thing had happened during the night, so wonderful, in fact, that one cannot be surprised that he thought
it unreal.

From the bazaar to the very gate of the palace was a
broad, smooth road. On each side were brick walls
covered with the whitest of cement, and decorated with
the heads of lions, and two large griffins, built of brick
and covered also with cement, guarded the entrance.
They were more than twelve cubits high ; their mouths
were wide open and showed their terrible fangs, and
their eyes looked upon the king with a stony glare.
The road was paved with blocks of stone cut as smooth
and laid as true as the cells of a honeycomb. There
was one road for men, one for oxen, and yet another
for horses. *Zayats* had been built here and there so
that travelers aweary could rest and be thankful, and
over all was a wide canopy of white cloth that extended
entirely from end to end and from side to side to pro-
tect the king from the sun when he should move along
the road to observe its wonders more closely.

In utter amazement he beat the gong that hung ready
to his side with such vigor that *amats*, soldiers, attendants, and the people from the city, came rushing out of
their houses to the palace gates expecting at least that
the neighboring prince with whom they had long been
at war had taken the city by surprise ; but they, like

the king, stood transfixed and speechless with wonder when they saw the road with its carvings and *zayats* and the canopy with the golden border spread above all.

The king called Myeh Khit. She came, and hidden in her turban was her son. The king had thought to punish this presumptuous woman by giving her an impossible task to do with a penalty that put her beyond the power of offending again, and was of course angry and disappointed that his scheme had been unsuccessful; but the occurrence had become the common talk of the market-place, and so he was obliged to carry out his part of the bargain, although it had gone contrary to his expectation and desires. So, much against his will, he called his daughter and gave an order that for seven days there was to be a feast in honor of the marriage of the princess.

But when the rejoicings of the people were finished, Khit was not given permission to live in his father's palace but was sent with his wife and mother to live in the old house where he had been born.

Six days after the marriage there was a feast at the pagoda, and the six daughters of the king went in state.

They rode upon royal elephants; dancers danced before them; the golden umbrellas protected them from the sun; and everybody fell upon their knees and clasped their hands as the august personages went along. Their retinue filled the street when they stopped at the little house where their sister lived.

" O sister," they called, " are you coming to the

feast ? '' but the poor girl in great shame told them she
could not come, and when they had gone, she sat on the
floor with her face in her hands and gave way to her
grief.

While she was sobbing, her husband approached and
told her not to be sorrowful. "My father is the great
Lord Sa Kyah," said he, "and he will give me anything I ask, so do not say, 'I am ashamed to go, as I
have only a frog for a husband.' You shall yet see
your proud father and unkind sisters bowing before
you and offering you presents as they offer to gods."

Seeing how distressed the poor girl really was, the
Lord Sa Kyah took pity on them and descended to
earth. He brought with him wonderful white clothes
such as the *hpeas* wear. They were brighter than the
stars that shoot across the sky at night, or the lightning
that flashes over the heavens during the hot season.
He also gave them a magic stone, which if placed under
their tongues, would enable them to fly wherever they
wished.

The next morning was the last day of the feast when
the boat races would be rowed, when the horses of the
king and his chief *amats* would race for prizes, when
the best jugglers would show their most wonderful
tricks, and the best dancers would dance under the
booths. In the midst of the fun and excitement a great
shout rent the air : "The mighty Lord Sa Kyah is de-
scending !" and right in the middle of the feasting
there was a flash of brilliant light and two wonderful
beings alighted. They were clothed in dazzling white,

and flew swifter than when a kingfisher darts from a tree toward its prey in the water.

Every one came crowding around as near as they dared, and upon their knees offered presents of food to the wonderful beings.

First and foremost came the princesses, who bowed till their foreheads touched the dust ; they lifted their clasped hands over their heads and turned away their faces while they offered the sweetest and most savory food to the visitors.   But it was noticed that although the spirits ate the food offered by the *amats* and common people, they would not eat that given by the princesses, but wrapped it up and placed it on one side.

The next day the princesses came to their sister's house and derided her.   " O wife of an animal," they cried, "you would not come to the feast, and so you lost the chance of seeing the mighty Lord Sa Kyah descend from the *hpea* country," and then they told of the wonderful sight, and again made fun of their unfortunate sister.

Khit's wife smiled at them and then she said : " It is you who are unfortunate, not I.   My husband is not the ugly animal you think him to be, but is a great and powerful *hpea*.   It was not the Lord Sa Kyah who descended yesterday, but his son, my husband, and myself, and to prove my words, whose are these ? " and she produced the very bundles of food that her sisters had offered the day before to the supposed ruler of all spirits.

The sisters were surprised to see that she had the

food there, but they laughed her to scorn when she told them of her husband.

In order that his son should become mighty and famous, the Lord Sa Kyah sent one of his attendants to the king, and caused him to give an order to his children that they should have a boat race. The one who reached the winning post first and carried away the flag on its rattan pole was to be king in his room, and the one who came in last was to be slave to the fortunate one.

There were great preparations among the servants of the six princesses, and many wagers were made as to who would be successful, but none wished to wager as to who would come in last, as all knew it would be the youngest sister.

"She has no boat," said they, "and has no servants to make one, or money to buy one. Even if she had, what could she do? Her husband has no hands, how could he row against and defeat the swift boatmen who have been called by the princesses?"

The king gave seven days in which his daughters were to prepare for the race, and during that time the shouting of the various crews as they practised on the lake was heard from early morning till the sun dropped behind the mountains, but only six boats were seen.

The race was to take place on a lake at the outskirts of the city, and on the morning of the seventh day, when the six princesses took their stations they were surprised to see that there was a seventh boat there, but they did not know that it was a magic boat sent by the

Lord Sa Kyah from the *hpea* country, and that the sixteen rowers were not men, but *hpeas*.

The course was over a thousand cubits to a post, around it, and return, and so fast did the magic boat glide through the water that it had covered the entire distance and the captain had laid the flag at the king's feet before any of the other boats had reached the first pole that showed half the distance.

But something even more wonderful than that had taken place. During the race, the time set apart during which the son of Myeh Khit was to have the form of a frog had expired, and, lo ! he was now the most handsome man in all the hill and water country. He had a crown of gold upon his head, and the magic white clothes such as only *hpeas* wear were on his person. His wife was clothed in as beautiful a manner, and the king, at last seeing the mistake he had made in treating him so badly, knelt on the shore and asked : " Which lord is the son of his slave ? " by which he meant, which of the lords was the one to whom he had given his daughter.

But the Lord Khit, as he was now called, did not take a mean revenge on his unkind brothers and sisters, and when they came on their knees begging for their lives, and asking the privilege of being his slaves, he took compassion on them, and instead of ordering them to immediate execution, made them his *amats*.

This is why the Shans who live in the hill and water country worship Sau Maha Khit.

HOW BOH HAN ME GOT HIS TITLE.

BOH HAN ME was one of the greatest generals who ever lived in the hill and water country. Just what his original name was nobody knows now, but this story tells how he gained his title.

One day he went into the jungle with his wife and his two children to gather *nau*, which is a kind of *puc* made from the young bamboo shoots. They were very successful in getting it, and were just on the point of going home with their loads, when right before them appeared a large black bear. The bear opened wide his mouth and roared, showing his immense white teeth and great throat, and came ambling toward them growling all the while in the fiercest kind of way.

Now as soon as the man saw the bear he just threw away all the *nau* that he had in his hands and ran for his life, calling on his wife to do the same. The two children followed their father and left their mother to get out of her trouble as best she could. She, however, was as brave as her husband was cowardly, and instead of running away, she took a handful of the longest of the shoots and thrust them down the open throat of the bear and killed him. She then took the short sword that they had brought from home to cut the shoots, and with it she skinned the bear, cut him up, and made the skin into a sack in which to carry the meat.

19

Meanwhile her cowardly husband did not stop running till he reached the city in which he lived, and then he told all his neighbors how he had been in the jungle and a great bear had attacked them ; how he had fought bravely for a long while, but at last it had killed his wife and eaten her.   The neighbors were very sorry for him, but advised him to get home and fasten all the doors and windows before the spirit of his wife would have time to get in, for they said, seeing that she was killed when he was with her, her ghost would without doubt try and gain admittance to the house and haunt it.   Once in, it would be very difficult to get her out.

The man, more frightened than ever, ran home as fast as he could and called his children to bring all the rice that was already cooked into the house, and then they fastened up the two doors and the one window with bamboos and rattan.   There was to be a feast in the city that night, and the two children wanted to go and see the fun, but their father was in such a fright that he would not give them permission to go, or even to look out through the holes in the sides of the house where the bamboo matting had come unfastened and bulged away from the posts.

By this time the sun had set and it was just getting dark, and the man, tired with the hunt in the jungle and the excitement after, was just going to sleep when he heard a voice that he recognized as his wife's calling to be let in.

"Husband, *oie !* " it called, " open the door and let me in.   I am very tired and hungry, and want rice and sleep. Get up quickly. Why have you fastened up the window and doors with bamboos and rattan? There are no bad men around; any one would think you were afraid thieves were coming to-night."

The man was frightened almost to death when he heard his wife's voice, for he felt sure it was her ghost coming to haunt him, so he called out:

"Ghost of my wife, *oie!* I will not let you in. If I did I would never be able to get you out again. You want to haunt this house. I will not let you in. Go away, go away!"

In vain the woman told him that she was indeed his wife, that she was not a ghost at all, but had killed the bear and had his skin on her back with the meat in it, and begged to be let in; the man would not believe her and so she had to wait outside. All night long she called and begged her husband to let her in, but in vain. When the sun had risen, however, he felt a little braver, and so he put his head out through the thatch, and saw that it really was his wife and not her ghost. With great joy he ran down, opened the door, and let her in, but when his wife told him how she had killed the bear, he again became frightened.

"We have arrived at great trouble," said he. "When the people hear that you have killed a bear, they will most surely kill you. What shall we do to escape and be freed from the impending punishment?"

But his wife was a clever woman, and when the neighbors came in to ask how it was that she had not been killed, she told a wonderful story, how through

the bravery of her husband she had been saved ; that
he had seen the bear, and by his bravery, that was so
great it was good to marvel at, it had been driven off.
The neighbors were very pleased that so brave a man
lived in their quarter, and he became famous, people
calling him Gon Han Me, or " the man who saw the
bear."

Gon Han Me was very proud of his title, as many
other vain people have been proud of titles they never
earned, but it came near costing him his life, and this
was the way it led him into great danger.   One day a
large cobra fell into the well that was in the yard before the chief door of the king's palace, and everybody
was afraid to draw water because of it.   When the
amats told the king that a cobra was in the well, he
gave orders that it was to be taken out, but nobody was
brave enough to go down the well and kill the snake.
The chief *amat* was in great distress.   He feared the
king would deprive him of his office if the snake were
not killed immediately.   He was not brave enough to
descend himself, and money, promises, and threats were
of no avail to induce any one else to go.   Everybody
declined to take the risk, and said : " Of what use is
money, or horses, or buffaloes, to a man bitten by a
cobra?   Will that free him from death?   Nay, go
yourself."

The poor *amat* was at his wits' end, when at last one
of the attendants told the king that in the quarter of
the city where his sister lived, was a man so brave that
he was called Gon Han Me, and said he : " If a man is

brave enough to see a bear in the jungle and not be afraid, surely he will dare go down the well and kill the cobra.''

The king was much pleased with the attendant for showing a way out of the difficulty. '' He surely is the man we want,'' said he ; '' go and call him immediately to come and destroy the snake.''

The attendant of the king came to Gon Han Me and said : '' Brother, *oie !* the king has heard that you are a very brave man, so brave, in fact, that your neighbors all talk of you and you have arrived at the rank of being called 'Gon Han Me.' Now in the royal well there is a snake, a cobra, which as you know is called the worst snake that lives. It is a very wicked snake and everybody has arrived at great trouble because of it. Nobody dares draw water there, and the king has given orders that it is to be killed. However, no one at the palace is brave enough to descend the well and kill the snake, but when his majesty heard of your great bravery, he sent me to order you to come immediately, descend the well, and kill the cobra. He will give you great rewards, and besides will make you a *boh* (officer) in the royal army.''

When Gon Han Me heard this he was in great distress and called his wife. '' Wife, *oie !* '' he said ; '' this unlucky name will certainly be the cause of my death. It will truly kill me. The king has called me to descend the royal well and kill a wicked snake that is frightening everybody in the palace. I am not brave enough to go. If I do not go, the king will have me

executed. I shall be killed whichever I do. If I go
the snake will kill me, if I do not go the king will kill
me. I shall arrive at destruction, and all because of
this miserable name.''

The wife pondered awhile and then advised her husband to get dressed in his best clothes and go to the
palace, look down the well to see what it was like, then
make some excuse to come back home and she would
tell him what next to do.

The man was soon dressed in his best clothes, and
was already going down the steps of the house when his
wife called out that he had left his *hsan* behind him.
Now when the Shans go into the jungle, or on a journey,
they carry with them a rice-bag, or *hsan*. This is a long
narrow bag, more like a footless hose than anything
else, and when filled with rice it is worn around the
waist, where it looks like a big snake coiled around.
Now Gon Han Me was very proud of his rice-bag, for
instead of being made of plain white cloth, as is the custom, it was embroidered all over with different colored
wools, and was so long that it went around his waist
several times.

He was so excited and terrified that when he reached
the well he did not notice that one end had been unfastened and was dragging on the ground, and as he
went to the well to look over, it caught around his legs,
overbalanced him, and he went head first into the well
with a tremendous splash. The next instant the snake
lifting its head darted at him, and all that the men
above, who were waiting with breathless interest to dis-

cover how the battle would end, could hear, was an in-
finite amount of splashing, yells, and hissing. Gon
Han Me never knew how it was, but in the fall his *hsan*
became twisted around the neck of the snake, and in a
few minutes it was choked to death.

The man for a while could hardly believe that the
snake was really dead. It seemed too good to be true,
but he came to the conclusion that his *kam* [1] was good,
and he would yet be a great and famous man. He
therefore assumed a heroic air, and at the top of his
voice called to the men at the mouth of the well :

"Brethren, *oie !* I have killed the snake and thus
freed you from the great danger from which you were
suffering. I will now throw up the end of this long
rice-bag. Do you catch it and pull me and the dead
snake up to dry ground.'' He thereupon threw up the
end of the embroidered *hsan*, the men caught it, and
the next minute he appeared with the dead snake in his
hand.

The king was very pleased with Gon Han Me for his
brave act. He gave him great rewards as he had promised, and also gave order that in future he should be
known by the name of ''Boh Han Me,'' or ''the officer
who saw the bear.''

Some time after this there was war between the king
and the ruler of the next province. There was a great
council called and it was unanimously agreed that as
Boh Han Me was the bravest man in the country, he
should be appointed as commander-in-chief.

---

[1] *Kam*, luck, or fate.

When the message came to his house, however, it caused him great distress, for as he told his wife, he did not want to be killed in the least ; he did not wish to run the risk of being killed or even hurt. Besides he had never been on horseback in his life. He had a buffalo that ploughed his fields, and it is true that occasionally, tired with the day's work, he had ridden home on its back when the sun sank into the west, but he was sure that if he got on the back of a horse it would immediately divine that he was ignorant of the art of riding, did not *mau* as he said, and he would be thrown to the ground and hurt, killed maybe. Who could tell ?

Again his clever wife came to the rescue. "You must go to the fight whether you want to or not," said she. "The king has given orders and he must be obeyed. To disobey the king is more dangerous than seeing a bear or even fighting a snake, so go you must. As to riding, that is easily managed. Bring your pony here and I will show you how to ride without danger."

On the never-to-be-forgotten day when the whole family went into the jungle to gather *nau*, they were very poor, but since the fight with the snake in the well, they had become rich, and so now the *boh* had servants to do his bidding, and he therefore called one of them to saddle his pony and bring it to the door of his house. This was soon done. He took his seat, and then his wife took long pieces of rawhide and fastened his legs, from ankle to knee, on both sides to the stirrups and girths. She knotted them securely so that there would

be no chance of his falling off his steed. He was very
pleased that he had such a clever wife, who could help
him out of every trouble into which he might fall, and
rode away well pleased with himself, and soon reached
the place where the soldiers were assembled awaiting his
appearance before beginning the march.

To have seen him nobody would have thought that
he was frightened sick. He sat up bravely, and you
would have thought that he was the best horseman in
all the hill and water country, but all the time he was
turning over in his mind the advice given by his wife
when they talked it over the night before. This was
what she said to him : " Now, when you get to the soldiers, see them start off. Give all the orders in a very
loud, pompous tone. Talk high, and and they will think
you *mau* very much (are very clever). Then you can
easily find some excuse to get to the rear, and you must
stay there till the fighting is all finished."

There was one party to this arrangement, however,
that they had both failed to take into account when
making their plans, and that was the pony. They
neither remembered that there was a possibility of the
pony taking it into his head to carry his master where
the latter did not want to go, but that was just what
happened, for, when the pony saw all the other horses
and the men marching off, he too commenced to move
forward. He was a fine big pony and was accustomed
to head processions, not to come at the tail end, and so
he started off of his own accord. Now we have said that
his rider had never been on horseback before, but had

often ridden his buffalo from the paddy field when the day's work of ploughing was over. When a man on a buffalo wishes to stop, he jerks the rope that is fastened to the animal's nose, and obedient to the signal, it stops. So, when the *boh* found his steed forging ahead a little faster than suited him, he jerked the reins, expecting the pony to stop, but to his consternation, he found it go all the faster. He jerked harder, the pony broke into a quick trot. He jerked again, the pony began to gallop. He was now thoroughly frightened and called out at the top of his voice, but this only frightened the pony more and it began to gallop just as fast as ever it could, and worse than all, it headed straight for the enemies' soldiers, whom he could see in the distance getting ready to receive him. He cursed his wife with all his heart. If he could only fall off! She had taken too good precautions against that. He pulled and tugged, but the rawhide was strong ; the knots were too tight ; and every minute brought him nearer to his enemies. He could hear the shouts of his friends in the distance getting fainter and fainter as the distance increased, calling him to come back. How he wished he could ! He swayed from side to side, first on one flank then on the other. The pony now had its head down between its knees, the bit between its teeth, and was tearing along like the wind. It would be hard to say which was the more frightened, the horse or its rider ; each frightened the other. But there was a lower depth yet to be reached. In jumping over a hole the saddle slipped to the side, the next instant away it

went, turned, and saddle, rider, and all slipped clear
around, and Boh Han Me found himself still securely
lashed to the saddle, squarely under his horse instead
of on it.

Meanwhile in the camp of the enemy a council of war
was being held. "Can any one tell me," asked the
king, "who commands our foes?"

"Our lord," said one of the *amats*, "it is a man who
has been picked out of the whole army, and is the
bravest man who ever drew a sword. He is called Boh
Han Me because he conquered a great fierce bear in the
jungle. He also went down a well in the royal palace
and killed the largest and fiercest snake ever seen in all
the hill and water country."

The king was much disquieted when he heard of the
prowess of this man, and was pondering whether it
would not be better to fight with silver than steel, and
offer a great reward to any man in the enemies' camp
who would bring to him the head of this doughty soldier, when he heard a great shout. He sprang to the
tent door and looked anxiously out. All eyes were
bent in one direction and a look of intense wonder, not
unmixed with fear, sat on each face. The king naturally expected to see the whole army of the enemy approaching in overwhelming numbers, but he shared the
wonder of his soldiers when he saw, not an army, but
one single man dashing toward him. The next instant
the rider disappeared entirely, but the horse came on
faster than before. Next instant there was the rider
again, arms tossing in the air, hair streaming behind,

only to disappear the following moment in the same mysterious way.

The face of the king blanched with terror as he asked in a whisper, "Who is this man?"

A hundred voices cried: "It is Boh Han Me, the bravest man alive! He has some charm that makes him invisible whenever he wishes, and he cannot be hurt by sword or arrow."

Nothing spreads so quickly as a panic, and almost before the king was aware of it, he was carried away in the fierce rush to escape. His men were blind with fear; they threw away their arms; men and officers fled for their lives, their only thought to flee from that horse and its terrible rider who disappeared and reappeared in such an awful fashion, and in a few minutes the field was deserted and the whole army in full retreat.

The horse by this time was exhausted. It stumbled, but regained its feet only to fall again immediately. It made another effort to struggle to its feet, but this time unsuccessfully, and then lay still on its side, its flanks heaving and its breath coming and going in quick sobs. Very cautiously Boh Han Me drew a knife and slowly cut one knot. The horse did not stir. Another followed, and soon one leg was freed. This made the task easier, and soon both legs were cut from their bonds and he sprang to his feet, bruised and sore, it is true, but no bones broken, and only too glad to be on solid earth again, and he vowed he would never from that day forth ever get on anything that moved faster than a buffalo.

What the king said when he reached the place where the foes had encamped may be imagined. He declared that a man as brave as his general had never lived in any age or country. For one man to charge a whole army, and, what was more, drive it off too, was a thing good to marvel at, and Boh Han Me did the wisest thing he ever did in his life, he just held his peace. When they had gathered together the spoil they returned home with the hero by the side of the king. The latter gave him a grand palace with gold, silver, oxen, buffaloes, elephants, and slaves in abundance, and also the rank of Boh Hoh Sök, which is the highest rank of general in the army, and means, "head of all the troops." The happy man lived many, many years, but he kept his promise, and whenever he wished to travel he rode upon an elephant and never again as long as he lived got upon the back of a horse.

THE TWO CHINAMEN.

AGES ago, when this world was new, having been created but a short while, two Chinese boys left their native country and started out on their travels to discover things new and strange. After wandering for many days they came to the hill and water country where the Shans live. Here they found a monastery, where lived very wise and learned priests, who instructed them in many ways.

They lived here some time and won the esteem of the head priest to such an extent that he showed them a magic sword and bow that had lain in the monastery many years waiting for somebody to carry away. The law was that the man who could bend the bow or could draw the sword from its sheath should keep it.

The elder brother went to the sword and tried to draw it. He pulled, he tugged, he strained, till the sweat ran down his face, but in vain. He could not draw it out one inch.

Seeing the ill success of his elder brother, the younger thought it impossible for him to draw the magic sword, but at his brother's command he took the handle in his hand and pulled with all his might. To everybody's surprise out came the magic sword, and the Chinaman walked away in triumph.

The elder brother now made up his mind that if he

32

could not get the sword he would try for the bow, and
he might have more success with that, so he exerted all
his strength, and slowly, slowly bent it, till the cord
was taut and the bow all ready to shoot.

The people of the city were amazed that the two
brothers should have such strength and good luck, and
many envious eyes followed them as they again set out
on their journey, carrying their trophies with them.

They traveled on and on till they gave up counting
the distance, it was so great, till one day, as they were
resting on the banks of a large river in a far country,
they saw a great fish swimming in the water. It was
so great that nobody heretofore had been able to catch
it, and it was in fact the king of all the fishes. It
broke all the nets and smashed all the traps. It
snapped all the lines that were set for it, and nobody was strong enough to pull it ashore when it did
take the hook. The Chinamen saw it, and the elder
brother instantly strung his bow, put on a bolt, and
shot the great fish as it was swimming in the shallow
water. In a few minutes he had it on his shoulder,
and they commenced to cross the bridge to the other
side of the river.

Now the river was very wide, the current was very
swift, and the bridge was not at all strong. It was
only made of bamboos and rattan and swung from side
to side as the men crossed it. When they got to the
middle it began to creak and strain till the two travelers were in great fear it would break. The one who
had killed it turned to his brother and said :

"O brother, the fish is so heavy I am afraid the bridge will break. Please draw your magic sword and cut it in halves, and then we will be able to get to the other side in safety."

The younger brother therefore drew his sword and cut the fish in halves; but he did not yet know how sharp the sword was, for he cut the fish in halves, it is true, but not only that, but the whole bridge as well, so that his brother fell into the water and was immediately swept from his sight. On his part he could not of course cross, now the bridge was down, so he returned to the same side of the river and ran along the bank looking to see whether his brother would be swept ashore in some shallow place; but although he ran till he was exhausted and then traveled for many days by the side of the river through the jungle, he could discover no trace of his lost brother.

Swiftly down the stream his brother was carried. He tried to swim first to one bank and then to the other as the current swept him along, but in vain. At last he gave up trying. Nobody knows just how long he was in the water, but for many days he floated, and when he was on the point of dying from exhaustion, cold, and hunger, his feet touched bottom, and, more dead than alive, he crawled up the bank to dry land.

He found that he had landed near a garden, and, on climbing over the wall, he discovered that it belonged to the king. He was too tired to climb back again, however, so sank on the ground and the next instant fell asleep from sheer weariness.

Now it happened that the king of that country had just died, and his *amats* had taken out the royal chariot and were drawing it around the city looking for the proper person to become king. As they went along they saw this young man sleeping in the royal garden with his magic bow beside him. He had come from nobody knew where. He was so strong that the river even could not kill him. Above all, he had a wonderful magic bow which none of the *amats* or nobles could bend, so they came to the conclusion that he indeed was the man who should be king of the country, and he was crowned with great pomp and magnificence.

The other brother had been left standing on the bridge when the elder fell into the water, as we have said, and for many days he followed the river bank till he too arrived in a far country. It was a very strange country. There were no men there, only monkeys, but they were the very cleverest monkeys that ever lived, and were ruled over by a *nang me prah*, that is, a queen, just as men are ruled. This queen of the monkeys fell in love with the Chinaman and married him, so that he became king of Monkey Land. They built a palace for him on the top of the highest tree in the jungle. Every seventh day they brought him food. Some brought plantains, some mangoes, some rice, and some fish fresh caught in the river.

The elder brother had now been king of the country where he had landed for some years, and one day he remembered his younger brother, whom he had left standing on the broken bridge with the sword in his

hand.   He therefore called his *amats* and told them he
was going on a long journey, and that they must rule
well and justly till he returned.   He then called his
favorite servants and set out to discover his brother.
They had a great store of provisions carried by coolies.
He had his royal elephants, on which he could ride
when traveling over the steep mountain roads and to
carry his chief queens, and ponies for riding over the
plains.

One night, however, he became separated from his
followers and lost his way.   He shouted and called, but
shouted and called in vain.   He could not find a trace
of them.   Servants, horses, elephants, and goods were
all gone, and he was in great fear that he would die in
the jungle.   When morning broke he was much surprised to see that he had arrived at a city, but that the
houses were all built on the tops of the trees, and on
looking closer, he discovered that instead of people
living in these houses the inhabitants were all large
monkeys.   Not a man was to be seen, and the monkeys
were very fierce and screamed at him in anger from the
top of every tree.   One especially he noticed as being
more fierce than any of the others, and he accordingly
leveled his magic bow and shot it dead.   As it fell
from the tree to the ground he heard all the friends of
the dead monkey come rushing out of their houses on
the tops of the trees calling to one another that a man
had killed one of their brethren, and asking that their
friends would come to kill the man who had been guilty
of the deed.

"The man standing at the top of the tree was the long-lost brother."   Page 37.

After a little time the king came to a tree that was taller than any other in the jungle, and upon it was a palace. Stairs led from the door of the palace to the ground, and as he looked more closely he saw a man up there. In great joy he called out to him, asking to be directed. "I am the king of a far country," he said, "and I am on a journey to search for my brother, whom I have not seen for many, many years. Last night I lost my way. Will you take pity on me and show me the way and I will give you a great reward?"

"Who was your brother?" asked the man in the tree.

"He was a Chinese student," returned the king, "and he had a wonderful magic sword. One day as we were traveling he cut a great fish in two, but such was the virtue residing in the magic sword that he not only cut the fish in halves but the bridge as well, so I left him standing on the end of the bridge."

You may imagine how pleased the king was when he discovered that the man standing at the top of the tree was the long-lost brother for whom he was searching, and he made ready to ascend to his house in the tree-top.

At that moment a little monkey ran down the tree toward him, and he kicked it aside, saying, "Out of my way, little monkey."

The small monkey in great anger said: "I am not a monkey, but your nephew."

"My nephew!" exclaimed the king in great astonishment. "What do you mean by that?"

His brother, the monkey king, then explained to him that he had married the queen of all the monkeys and that this was their child, that he ruled over all the monkeys, who had built this palace for him and every seventh day brought him tribute of food.

"I am sorry to say, then," said the elder brother, "that I have killed one of your subjects," and at the same moment the wife and son of the dead monkey approached their king.

"Our lord," said they, "the man yonder has been guilty of a great crime. He entered the domains of our lord and although we did nothing to him, yet he raised his bow and killed one of the servants of our lord. Therefore our lord's servants demand that he shall be killed too."

"I am very sorry," said the king of the monkeys, "that you have killed that special monkey. He was very clever and brave. He was also one of my chief *amats*, and his friends will assuredly kill you."

The monkeys were now assembling by hundreds and calling to each other everywhere. Every treetop appeared alive with angry figures all calling for vengeance on the man who had killed their friend.

The king, however, who had taken sides with his brother, was not afraid, and said he could kill all the monkeys in the country; and he drew his sword and cut in halves the monkey nearest to him. To his great surprise, however, the two halves of the monkey he had killed each became a whole monkey and attacked him again, so that he now had two to fight in-

stead of one. If he cut off the hand or leg of a
monkey with his long sword, it immediately turned
into two, and he soon saw that unless he devised some
other way of fighting them they would soon kill them
both.

He therefore rushed off to the jungle and got a great
hollow bamboo. He then went to a bees' nest and
swept all the bees into it, and caught a great many scor-
pions and centipedes, snakes and spiders. When the
monkeys came toward him to renew the fight, he opened
one end of the bamboo and the insects and reptiles,
swarming out, very angry at being kept prisoners in the
hollow bamboo, soon drove the monkeys off so that the
two brothers were able to escape. Shortly afterward
they found the escort of the king and together returned
to the city where the good elder brother made the
younger his chief *amat*.

Now when the younger brother became *amat*, he of
course saw what a great king his brother was. He saw
his subjects kneel before him ; he saw the royal elephants, oxen, horses, and buffaloes ; he saw the riches
in money, jewels, and goods that belonged to him ; that
his queens were the most beautiful women in the land ;
and he became jealous. Then he coveted all these
things. The next step was easy ; he determined to kill
his brother and become king in his stead. Then he
began to ponder and plot how best he could destroy the
brother who had been so good to him. He did not remember how that same brother had left all these things
to come and hunt for him ; how he had given **him**

riches and honor and position, so that now he was chief minister and next to him in power. No, he did not think of any of these things, but like the ungrateful man that he was, thought only that his brother had more than he.

He soon came to the conclusion that he could not kill his brother in the city, for everybody loved the king, and he feared that his crime would be discovered, so he was obliged to wait until they should be alone in the jungle together. The opportunity soon came. One day the king was out hunting and had gotten separated from all his followers. His brother the *amat* was a short distance ahead when he saw, just in front of him, a very deep hole, so deep in fact that it was impossible to see the bottom. In great excitement he turned and beckoned to the king as fast as he could, calling out in a loud voice that he had something very wonderful to show him.

The king thought that at least he had discovered a mountain of rubies and came running up. He knelt by the side of the hole but could see nothing.

"There is nothing down there," said he.

"Let our lord lean a little farther over," said the cunning *amat*. "He will then see the most wonderful thing in the world."

The king bent farther over and his wicked brother gave him a push that sent him headlong to the bottom.

He had now succeeded in all his plans; he had reached the height of his ambitions, but although he became king he was not happy. He had trouble all the time. It is true he had his brother's riches, that he rode the royal elephants, wore the royal robes, and lived in the royal palace, but he had trouble with his *amats*, with his soldiers, and his people, and therefore instead of being happy as he expected he would be, he was unhappy and miserable.

If he had only known what was happening in the jungle he would have been more anxious still. His brother was not dead as he thought. The fall to the bottom of the hole did not kill him and he was only a prisoner. His followers had all gone back to the city with his wicked brother. He called, but called in vain. He heard nothing but the echo of his own cries, and he was about to give up in despair, when it happened that the mighty Lord Sa Kyah coming through the jungle heard his cries and inquired the cause. The king did not know that this was the Lord Sa Kyah, but told him all that had happened. Lord Sa Kyah was very angry with the king's heartless brother and created at the bottom of the hole a lily of the kind that has a very long stalk. The king sat upon the blossom of the lily which then began to grow very rapidly, and as it grew carried the king up toward the mouth of the hole.

As he gradually rose toward daylight he saw that a tree was growing at the very edge of the pit, and that some of the branches hung over. He saw also that a monkey was busily engaged in feeding on the leaves and fruit. The lily, of course, made no noise as it pursued its upward path ; the king also kept quiet so as not to frighten the monkey, and when he was near enough suddenly put forth his hand and caught it by the tail. The monkey screamed and kicked, fought and scratched, but in vain ; the king held on, and at last the monkey climbed down the tree taking the king with him, and the latter was speedily standing once more on solid ground and able to offer up his thanks to the mighty Lord Sa Kyah.

The king was not long in reaching the city and when he arrived, to his great sorrow he saw, as he expected, his ungrateful brother reigning, while the people all sorrowed for their old king. He determined to wait awhile before he declared himself, feeling that the Lord Sa Kyah who had already once helped him when in trouble and danger would aid him in regaining his lost kingdom ; so he went into the poorest part of the city, put on the poorest and most ragged clothes that he could find, and sat near the gate of the city begging, from whence he often saw his brother riding by in state.

One day the heralds came riding by and stood in the open space fronting the market where the gambling booths are, and gave notice that the king had commanded that if anybody could bend the magic bow belonging to the late king, his brother, he was to be made the chief *amat* of the kingdom and receive many and great presents besides.

As may be imagined, the next day there was a great crowd gathered together at the great gate of the palace, waiting for the king. At last out he came with all his ministers and followed by attendants bearing golden umbrellas. Behind him came a soldier carrying over his shoulder the magic bow which was placed at the king's feet. The king called upon his soldiers to come and bend the bow, and the strongest of them came forward, but although they pulled and tugged, tugged and strained, they could not bend it. Then the people of the city, or "the king's people," as they loved to call themselves in contradistinction to the people who lived in the jungle villages, tried, but met with no better success than the soldiers. They could not bend the bow. The king then ordered the *amat löng* to call the men from the jungle. The very strongest coolies, those who carried heavy burdens over the mountains, came in answer to the king's summons, but although some of them could carry fifty *soie* over the highest mountain they could not draw the cord a hand's-breadth.

The king, much disappointed, was about to return to the palace when a beggar man approached and bowing at his feet said he was able to draw the bow and fire an arrow from it. The king was angry at what he thought was the presumption of this beggar. The soldiers derided him, saying that the bravest of them could not draw the bow and how was a beggar to do it? The coolies also asked him whether he could carry fifty *soie* over Loi Mawk Pah that was called the Cloud Mountain, because its head was often in the clouds. But the beggar asked to be allowed to try and the king gave orders that he should be given the bow, at the same saying that he assuredly should be made *amat löng* if he was successful, but if he could not bend the bow, he should be put to death immediately.

The beggar assented to these terms and seized the bow. He took hold of the string and without any show of strength pulled it a hand's-breadth, and then as the king and his courtiers looked on in amazement he pulled it to its full length, placed the string on the ivory trigger, put an arrow on it, and asked the king where he should shoot.

"Straight up into the air," said the king. The beggar raised the bow, twang went the string, and the arrow whizzed out of sight. Everybody stood looking up into the sky when suddenly one of the courtiers gave a warning cry. It came too late. The arrow had gone straight up, turned, and fell almost on the same spot from whence it was shot. Almost, but not quite, for in its fall it struck the upturned face of the king and he fell dead.

A great cry was raised as the king fell and the guards rushed forward to seize the beggar and lead him to immediate execution, but he waved them off with a gesture of his hand. The next instant his rags fell from him and he stood before them in the royal robes of a king.

Thus we see that the younger brother, although indeed he had not murdered his brother the king, yet did kill him in his thoughts and intentions, and he suffered the punishment that is always meted out to the man who kills his fellow.

STORY OF THE PRINCESS NANG KAM UNG

THERE was once a king who reigned over one of the largest States in the hill and water country. For a long time there had been war between him and the *sau hpa* of the neighboring State, but at last his soldiers had been successful, and his enemy had been driven out of his possessions, which had thereupon been added to his own. A great feast had been given when his soldiers returned to their homes, and he was now sitting with his queens and his seven daughters in the palace watching a performance given in honor of the victory. He praised the actors for their skill, and then asked his daughters whether they had enjoyed the performance. They one and all assured him that they had enjoyed it much, and then turning to them he continued :

"That is right, my daughters, enjoy yourselves to-day and to-morrow and all through your lives. You are the daughters of a mighty king, and it is your lot to be happy and enjoy yourselves all your lives, therefore again I say enjoy yourselves and be happy."

The eldest of the daughters, who was a perfect courtier said : "O our lord, our luck is fortunate, because it depends on that of the lord our father, and who is so fortunate as he ? "

The king was very pleased with the flattery of his

45

daughter, and promised to grant any request she would make of him.

The youngest daughter, however, was young and foolish, and had not yet learned the truth that in a king's presence it is not well always to say what one thinks, and therefore she said to her sister: "Your luck may depend on the luck of the lord our father, but mine is my own and depends upon myself alone."

When the king heard this he was very angry that one of his daughters, and she the youngest too, should have the presumption to say that she depended for anything at all on any other than he, and he determined to punish her.

For a long time he pondered on the best way to do this and at last devised a plan which, if severe, was at least novel.

He called his *amats* to go throughout the whole land and search for the poorest man in all his kingdom, and when they had found him they were to bring him to the palace and he would marry his youngest daughter to him, and then, said he, "We will see about luck after that."

Day after day the heralds searched the land but they could not find a man poor enough to suit the king. All who were brought before him acknowledged that they had something valuable, either a little money, a precious stone, or a distant relative who was rich and from whom they could borrow a little if necessary. A man of this description would not suit the angry king. He wanted one poorer than that.

At last the *amat löng*, or chief minister, brought a man before him and said that he was the poorest in all the land. His name was Ai Du Ka Ta. He was a woodseller in the bazaar, who every day went into the jungle and picked up the dead branches of the trees that had fallen to the ground, and brought them to the market every fifth day to sell. So poor was he that he did not even own the sword that is the almost insep- arable companion of the Shan and is used, among other things, to cut down the small trees that are left to dry for firewood, so he had to be content to pick up the small branches that he found under the trees, and got a proportionately small price when he carried his load into the bazaar.

When he appeared before the king, his trousers were all fringed at the bottom where they had been torn by the thorns in the jungle. His turban months before had been white, but now it was a deep gray ; it was only half its original length and was full of holes. Jacket he had none, and when the king asked him how many blankets he had upon his bed at home to keep him warm at night when the cold wind brought the rain up the valley, he answered sorrowfully, " Not one, our lord." He had no relative except an old mother whom he was obliged to support, and who was known through- out the district in which she lived as the woman with the bitterest tongue in all the land, and when too sick to move from her mat, she would yet fill the air with poisoned words.

The king was very pleased with his *amat löng* for

finding Ai Du Ka Ta, and gave him a very fine horse as a reward. Then he called his daughter, took away all her fine clothes and married her to this poorest man in his realm and drove her out of the palace amid the jeers and taunts of the very people who, before her disgrace, had waited upon her every word and had done her bidding while they trembled before her. The king also took away her old name and commanded that in future she was to be known as Nang Kam Ung, which means, " The woman whose luck depends upon herself."

The house, or rather hut, to which Ai Du Ka Ta took his bride was in the jungle. It was only four bamboo poles stuck in the ground and covered with dried grass and bushes. Not even a sleeping mat was on the ground—there was no floor—and the chattie in which he cooked his rice had a hole in it, and had to be set upon three stones sideways over the fire with the hole uppermost, to prevent the water leaking and putting out the fire.

Fortunately the girl's mother had helped her to smuggle out her " birth-stone," which was a large, valuable ruby, and so she took it off her finger and gave it to her husband, telling him to go and sell it and buy clothes and food for both of them.

Ai looked at the stone and said, " Who will give me food and clothes for a little red stone like that? We have no fools or mad men living near here who would do such a foolish thing as that," for you must remember he had lived in the jungle all his life, and had never heard of precious stones, much less seen one till now.

His friends were just as ignorant of its value as he was. He went from house to house in the little village near, but all laughed at him till he became disgusted, threw the stone away in the jungle and came home in a very ill humor with his wife for leading him such a wild-goose chase, and making him appear foolish in the eyes of the few people he knew.

His wife was in great distress when she found that he had thrown the ruby away, and told her husband that if he had gone to the city and taken it to the jewelers, instead of to the ignorant people in the jungle, they would have given him in return enough money to keep them in food and clothing all the hot season and build a new house into the bargain.

Ai looked at her and said : '' Indeed, that is a thing good to marvel at. Why, I know where there are coolie-basket loads of such red stones in the dry bed of a river near where I gather sticks for fire-wood in the jungle, waiting for anybody to carry away, and I never thought them worth the labor of taking to the bazaar.''

The princess was full of joy when she heard this, and the next morning they borrowed two coolie baskets from a man in the village. Bright and early they went to the river bed, and there, even as Ai had said, were basket loads of fine rubies. They gathered them up carefully and buried most of them, covering over the hole with a flat stone, so that no one would discover their hoard, and then the princess, picking out a double handful of the largest and clearest ones, sent them to her father.

D

The king, when he saw the jewels, instead of being pleased, fell into a great passion, called the unfortunate *amat löng* into his presence, and after rating him soundly, deprived him of all his goods, houses, and lands, deposed him from office, and drove him from his presence as poor as Ai himself had been.

"I ordered you to call a poor man," roared the king to the trembling man before him. "I said he was to have no goods or property at all, and here the very next day he sends me a double handful of the very best rubies I ever saw in my life."

In vain the culprit assured the king that the day before Ai was certainly the poorest man in the whole kingdom, and complained that the jewels must have been the work of some *hpea*, whom he had unwittingly offended, and who had therefore determined on his ruin in revenge. The king would listen to no excuse, and the unhappy *amat* was glad to crawl from his presence before resentment had carried him to the length of ordering his execution.

The very next night a wonderful golden deer entered the royal garden where the king was accustomed to sit when it became too warm in the palace, and after doing an immense amount of mischief, eating favorite flowers, and otherwise destroying and ruining the garden, it leaped over the fence and disappeared in the early morning fog, just as the guards were arousing themselves from sleep. It was in truth not a golden deer as the guards had told the king, but a *hpea* that had assumed this form; but the king not knowing this ordered his heralds to go through the city immediately and call upon all the inhabitants to come early next morning to help their lord catch it. Ai was summoned with the rest of the people. He had no horse, but going to the city gate that day he saw that a race between horses belonging to the king was about to be run. Ai was a good horseman, and asked the head horse-feeder of the king to let him ride one of the animals. He rode, and rode so well that he won the race, and that official was so pleased with him that he promised to grant him any request in his power. Ai asked for the privilege of riding the same horse at the hunt next day, and the request was readily granted, and thus it happened that, next morning when he went to the place appointed, he rode a horse that was faster than any other there except the one the king himself rode.

The people were divided into four parties ; one toward the north, one toward the south, one east, and one west. The king stationed himself with the party at south, and the *amats* were at the north, and when the deer was at last driven out of the jungle by the beaters it headed toward the king and dashed by him at great speed.

The *hpea* that had taken the form of the deer wished to have some fun at the king's expense, and therefore kept ahead just where the king could see him all the while, sometimes but a cubit or two away from him, and then when the country was open, darting far in advance. So swiftly did they go that in a few minutes the men on foot were left behind, and after a while all except those upon the very fastest horses were distanced, till at last only the king and Ai were left, the latter but a little behind the king. All day long the chase continued till, just as the sun was setting and men and horses were both exhausted, the deer made straight for a precipice that appeared to block the path on each hand as far as the eye could reach. The king was congratulating himself that the deer could not possibly escape now, when he saw right before him an opening in the rock, and the next instant the *hpea* disappeared in the cave and the king was obliged to give up the chase, for even if his horse could have carried him any farther, which it could not, the cave was so dark that nothing could be seen inside.

The king fell from his horse almost dead with fatigue, and managed to crawl under a wide-spreading banyan tree that grew near. The only other person there was Ai, and he, coming to the king, massaged his limbs till the tired monarch fell asleep. After a while he awoke and Ai asked him to eat some rice he had prepared, but the king said he was too tired to eat anything; but at last he managed to eat a little sweet, glutinous rice that the princess had cooked in a hollow piece of bamboo and given to her husband before he set out that morning.

The king was very grateful and asked Ai his name; but the latter was afraid to tell what his real name was, so, as his mother years before had been in the habit of selling betel-nut in the bazaar, he told the king that his name was Sau Boo, or betel-nut seller.

The king was very pleased with him and promised
him great rewards when they got back to the palace;
but in a few minutes he had dropped asleep again, and
Ai sat alone keeping guard.

It was very fortunate that he too did not go to sleep,
for as every one knows, the banyan is a sacred tree,
and this one was inhabited by a *hpea* who was noted
for being one of the cruelest and most dreaded spirits in
all the land. Ai roused the king and told him there
was a *hpea* in the tree and begged him not to sleep
there for it would assuredly kill them both before morning.

The king said, "Wake me not, trouble me not.
From my head to my feet, I am nothing but aches and
pains. Were I to move I should die. I may as well
die at the hands of the *hpea*." So saying he fell asleep
again, and Ai did not dare to disturb him, but watched
all night long.

During the night Ai heard the *hpea* grumbling to
himself several times and promising himself the pleasure
of killing them on the morrow, so he pretended to be
asleep so that he could hear what the *hpea* said and if
possible thwart him.

"These mortals have presumed to sleep under my
tree," he heard him say, "but it shall be the last time
they sleep anywhere. Let me see," he continued,
"how shall I kill them? Which will be the best way?
Ah, I know. Early to-morrow when they get ready to
leave, I will break the tree in two, and the top shall
fall on them. If, however, they escape, I will saw

through the supports of the first bridge, so that it will break when they are in the middle, and they will fall to the bottom of the valley below. Then if that should fail, I will loosen the stones of the arch of the city gate so that it will fall on them as they pass underneath, and if that does not kill them, when the king arrives at his palace and being thirsty with his long ride calls for water, I will change the water in the goblet to sharp needles that will stick in his throat and kill him. If he does not drink the water, however, he will assuredly be very tired and will go to sleep immediately, and I will send an immense rat into his room that will kill him without doubt.''

Having finished making his plans, the *hpea* left the tree and started the work of preparing the different traps for the mortals who had enraged his hpeaship by daring to sleep under the tree, and thus profane his home.

The king was frightened half to death when he awoke next morning, and found that he had been sleeping all night under the tree of that special *hpea;* but Ai, or Sau Boo as the king called him, told him not to be frightened for he could save his life if the king would only follow his advice and do as he told him.

The king promised to follow his words implicitly, and also promised him unheard-of rewards if he only helped him to get to his palace in safety.

The first danger was the tree, and so Ai got their horses ready and under the pretense of allowing them to eat grass before setting out on their journey, he gradually worked them nearer and still nearer the edge of the tree, and then, with one bound, they both galloped out from under it. At the same instant there was a great crash and the whole top of the tree fell to the ground. So near did it fall on them that the king's turban was torn from his head by one of the upper branches, but beyond this no harm was done.

Next, instead of riding over the bridge, they went along the bank a little distance, and soon found a place where the *hük* was narrow and leaped their horses to the other side. While they were jumping, Ai threw a heavy stone he had brought with him on to the bridge, and the *hpea*, who fortunately was near-sighted, thinking it was the tread of the horses, broke it down, so that fell into the water fifty feet below, but the king and his follower were safe on the other side.

The next danger was the city gate. They walked their ponies slowly as though they were very tired, till they came to within a cubit of the gate, and then galloped through at the top of their speed, and crash went the gateway behind them. They were covered with dust but not hurt.

The king was very thankful to have arrived at his palace and being very thirsty with the journey and excitement, as the cunning *hpea* had expected, called for a drink of water, but ere he could place the cup to his lips his faithful follower turned it upside down, and instead of water, out fell a cupful of sharp needles, and again the king's life was saved.

Worn out with his ride he told his servants to prepare his room as he would sleep. Ai called the chief guard and told him to have a lamp burning all night, to take his sharpest sword with him, and guard the king carefully. In the middle of the night when the tired king was sleeping soundly, into the room came creeping slowly, slowly, the biggest rat ever seen. It had long, sharp teeth and wicked glaring eyes, and made toward the king. But the guard, warned by Ai, was on the watch, and just as the rat was about to spring at the king's throat, the soldier with a sweep of his long, sharp sword cut off its head, and thus the king through the cleverness of one man escaped the last danger and could now live without fear.

The next morning the king called his heralds and bade them go into the city and summon Sau Boo to come to the palace to be rewarded. They searched and called, but searched and called in vain. No man ever heard of a man by that name, and the king was fast getting angry when the *amats* told him that they personally had gone to every house except one, and that was the house of Ai. The king in surprise ordered them to call his son-in-law. "He may be able to tell us something about him," he observed. Ai accordingly obeyed his summons, but the king was more surprised yet when Ai told him that Sau Boo and himself were one and the same, and that it was he who had rescued the king from so many dangers.

At first his father-in-law became angry and refused to believe him, but Ai gave an account of everything that had happened from the time when the deer broke cover, till the rat was killed by the guard, and thus convinced the king of his truthfulness.

The king then made a great feast, called all his ministers and generals together, and made a proclamation that Ai in future should be his *amat löng* and should be king when he himself died.

Thus did the princess prove that her luck really depended upon herself, and not on the king, and to-day we say, "May your luck be as good as the luck of Nang Kam Ung."

HOW THE HARE DECEIVED THE TIGER.

AT the beginning of the world a hare, tiger, ox,
buffalo, and horse became friends and lived together. One day the tiger was out hunting when, it
being in the middle of the hot season, the jungle caught
fire, and a strong wind blowing, it was not long before
the whole country was in flames. The tiger fled, but
the fire followed. Never mind how fast he ran, the
flames followed him, till he was in great fear of being
burned alive. As he was rushing along he saw the ox
feeding on the other side of the river and called out
to him :

"O friend ox, you see the fire is following me wherever I go. Where is a place of refuge that I can escape
the fire ?"

Now close to the tiger was a jungle full of dried
grass, such as the Shans use for thatching their houses,
and the ox replied, "Go to the grass jungle yonder, my
brother, and you will be safe."

But dried grass is the most inflammable thing in the
whole hill and water country, and so here, not only did
the flames follow the tiger, but they ran ahead of him
and threatened to engulf him on every side. In great
anger he roared at the ox, "False deceiver, if ever I
escape from this danger, I will return and kill you,"
but the ox only laughed at him and continued eating.

58

In desperation, the tiger leaped over the flames and found himself near the horse. "O friend horse," he cried, "where can I go? I am in great danger of being burned to death."

Now it happened that once the tiger had been very rude to the horse and called him many bad names, so now he thought this was a good opportunity to be revenged; so he said: "Yonder is a big bamboo jungle, run to that and you are safe"; but the tiger found that the horse was also a false friend, for the fire following him speedily ignited the tall bamboos which burned fiercely and falling from above, almost completely covered the poor beast.

At the beginning of the world the tiger was a beautiful yellow color, but the bamboos falling all over him, burnt him in stripes, and since that time his descendants have had long black stripes all over their coats.

"When I have escaped from this," yelled the angry tiger, "I will come back and kill you."

"Very good," sneered the horse, "and I will arch my neck so that you can get a good bite," but this was said to deceive the tiger, as the horse intended to lash out with his hind feet when the tiger came to fight him. Nevertheless, from that day the necks of all horses have been arched, and they cannot fight an enemy in front, but are obliged to arch their necks, lower their heads, and kick from behind.

The tiger, by this time tired to death and suffering from the burns of the bamboos, saw the buffalo and accosted him as he had his other friends.

"O good friend buffalo," he cried, "I am in great danger of being burned alive. The horse and the ox have not only deceived me, but in following their advice I have arrived at a worse condition than before. What can I do to be freed from this great danger?"

The buffalo looked up from the cool river where he was enjoying a bath, and taking compassion on him said: "If you will catch hold of my throat I will duck you in the river and so you shall escape from the danger that is following you."

So the tiger seized the good buffalo by the throat and was held under water till the fire had burnt itself out. The tiger was very grateful to the buffalo and made an agreement with him that from that time no tiger should ever kill a buffalo, and it is only the very worst tigers, those that kill men, that ever kill a buffalo, and the tigers that are guilty of killing buffaloes are sure to be killed themselves, sooner or later.

The tiger held so fast to the buffalo that when the latter came out of the water, his throat and neck were all white, and buffaloes all have that mark on their necks and throats till this very day.

The tiger was so cold after his bath that he shook and shivered as though he had fever, and seeing a little house made of dried grass a short distance off he went to it and found that a hare was living there.

"Good friend," said the tiger, "I am so cold I am afraid I shall die. Will you take compassion on me and allow me to rest in your house and get warm before I return home?"

"Come in, our lord," said the hare. "If our lord deigns to honor my poor house with his presence, he will confer a favor that his slave will never forget."

The tiger was only too glad to go into the hare's house, and the latter immediately made room for him by sitting on the roof. Soon the tiger heard click ! click ! click ! and he called out : "O friend hare, what are you doing up there on the roof of your house?"

Now the hare was really at that moment striking fire with her flint and steel, but she deceived the tiger and said, "It is very cold up here, and our lord's slave was shivering," but the next moment the spark struck the dried grass on the roof and the house was soon in flames.

The tiger dashed out just in time and turned in a rage on his late host, but the hare was far away, having jumped at the same moment that the spark set fire to the roof of the house.

The tiger gave chase, but after a while he saw the hare sitting down and watching something intently, so he asked, "What are you looking at?"

"This is a fine seat belonging to the Ruler of the Hares," returned she.

"I would like to sit on it," said the tiger.

"Well," said the hare, "wait till I can go and ask our lord to give you permission."

"All right, I will watch till you come back and will not kill you as I intended doing, if you get me permission to sit on it," said the tiger.

Now this was not a chair at all, but some hard sharp

stones that the hare had covered with mud and shaped with her paws to deceive the tiger. The hare ran off a long distance and pretended to talk with some one and then called out : "The lord of the chair says, our lord the tiger may sit, if he throws himself down upon it with all his might. This is our custom."

The tiger flung himself upon what he thought was the chair with all his might, but the soft mud gave way and he fell upon the stones underneath and hurt his paws badly. He therefore sprang up and vowed vengeance on the hare that he could just see far off in the distance.

By and by as the hare was running along she saw a large wasps' nest hanging from the branch of a tree, so she sat down and watched it intently. When the tiger came up he was so curious to know what the hare was looking at so intently that he did not kill her, but instead asked her what she was looking at.

The hare showed the tiger the wasps' nest on the tree and said: "That is the finest gong in all the hill and water country."

"I would like to beat it," said the tiger.

"Just wait a minute," returned the hare, "and I will go to the lord of the gong and ask permission for you to beat it."

The hare ran till she was far away in the jungle, and then at the top of her voice called out: "If you wish to beat the gong, the lord of the gong says you must strike it as hard as you can with your head. That is his custom."

"Again the cunning hare deceived the tiger."

Page 63.

The tiger butted at the nest with all his might and made a big jagged rent in its side, and out flew the angry wasps in swarms, completely covering the poor tiger, who with a dreadful yell of pain tore away from his tormentors. His face was all swollen, and from that day till the present, the faces of tigers have all been wide and flat.

Again he chased the hare, and when the smart from the stings of the wasps had subsided a little, he found to his great joy that he was gaining on his enemy fast. The hare on her part saw that the tiger would soon catch her and looked around for some means of escape, and spied just before her a snake half in and half out of its hole.

The hare stopped as before and sat gazing at the snake so intently that the tiger instead of killing her as he had intended to do, asked her what it was in the hole.

"This," returned the hare, "is a wonderful flute that only kings and nobles are allowed to play. Would our lord like to play?"

"Indeed I would," said the tiger; "but where is the lord of this wonderful flute? Whom shall I ask for permission?"

"If our lord watches right here," said the cunning hare, "his slave will go to the lord of the flute and ask permission," and the tiger, well content, sat down to wait.

Again the cunning hare deceived the tiger by pretending to ask permission, and when a long distance

off he called as before: "Our lord has permission to
play the flute. Let him put it in his mouth and blow
with all his might. This is the custom of the lord
of the flute."

The foolish tiger immediately took the snake's head
into his mouth, but the sound that followed came from
the tiger, not from the flute, and a terrible yell he gave
as the snake bit his mouth! But the hare was far
away and would soon have been safe but for an unlooked
for accident that nearly ended her life.

The people who lived in that part of the hill and
water country were at war with the State that joined
them on the north, and thinking that the soldiers of the
enemy would soon invade their country they had made
a trap in the middle of the path over which the hare
was running. First they dug a hole so deep that
should anybody fall in, it would be impossible to climb
out again. The sides of the pit were dug on the slant
so that the opening was smaller than the bottom. Over
the top they had placed thin strips of bamboo that would
break if any extra weight came upon them and they
had covered the whole with grass and leaves so that no
traveler would know that a trap was there. Into this
hole fell the poor little hare.

Presently the tiger came up to see where the hare had
gone, and when he saw the hole in the middle of the
path, he called out, "Where are you, friend hare?"
and the hare from the bottom of the trap called out,
"I have fallen into a trap."

Then the tiger sat on the ground and just bent double

with laughter to think that at last he had the hare in his power, but the little animal down in the hole although she did not say anything, thought harder in a few minutes than the tiger had in all his life. By and by as she looked up through the hole she had made in the roof, she saw that the sky overhead was getting darker and darker as a storm was coming on, so in great glee, although she pretended to be very much frightened, she called out as loudly as ever she could :

"Our lord tiger ! our lord tiger ! "

At first the tiger did not answer, so the hare then called, "Does not our lord see the great danger approaching ?   Let our lord look at the sky."

The tiger looked up and saw the dark clouds coming slowly, slowly on, covering the whole sky ; his laughter stopped and he soon began to get very frightened.

After a while, when it had become still darker, he called to the hare: "O friend, what is the matter with the sky ?   What is going to happen ? "

Then the hare replied: " Our lord, the sky has fallen where you see it is dark ; that is far away, but in a few minutes it will fall here and everybody will be crushed to death."

The foolish tiger was now frightened half to death and called to the hare: "O friend, I have treated you badly in trying to kill you.   Do not be angry and take revenge on me, but take compassion on my terrible condition, and graciously tell me how to escape this danger, and I swear that I will never try to harm you more."

It was the hare's turn to laugh now, but she only
E

laughed quietly to herself, for she was afraid the tiger
would hear her, then she said, " Down here our lord's
slave is quite safe.   If our lord descends, he too will be
safe," and before the hare had hardly finished, the
cowardly tiger made a jump for the hole the hare had
made and joined her at the bottom of the trap.

But the hare was not out yet and she began to plan
how she could get out herself and yet keep the tiger in.
At last a happy thought struck her.   She sidled up to
the tiger and began to tickle him in the ribs. The tiger
squirmed and twisted first one way and then the other,
first to one side and then to the other ; at last he could
stand it no longer and catching the hare he threw her
out of the trap and she landed on solid ground.

As soon as the hare found she was safe, she began to
call at the top of her voice: "O men, come ! come ! I,
the hare have deceived the tiger and he is at the bottom
of the trap.   O men, come !   I, the hare call you.
Bring your spears and guns ; bring your swords, and
kill the tiger that I have tricked into entering the trap."

At first the men did not believe the hare, for they did
not think that an animal so small as the hare could deceive the tiger, but then they also knew that the hare
was very clever and had much wisdom, so they brought
their spears and their guns, their swords and their
sticks, and killed the tiger in the trap.

Thus did the hare prove that though small she was
full of wisdom, and although the tiger was bigger,
stronger, and fiercer than she, yet she, through her
wisdom, was able to kill him.

THE STORY OF THE TORTOISE.

THERE was once a man who had two wives. Now as everybody knows it is always the chief wife that the husband loves best, while the other instead of being *Mae Long*, is only *Mae Noi*, and this often causes jealousy and trouble in the family. It was so in this case, especially as the chief wife did not have a son to add to her dignity. They each had a daughter, the name of the chief wife's child was Nang Hsen Gaw, and that of the other Nang E.

One day the husband of these women went to the lake to fish. He caught a large number of shell fish and put them on the shore for his wives to bring home. The younger took her share of the load, but, being very hungry, she ate them all. The mother of Nang Hsen Gaw, however, was not greedy like the other woman, and so she put all the fish that were left into her bag and began to trudge slowly toward the house.

Now, the mother of Nang E was a witch, although no one, of course, knew it. Being wicked enough to be a witch, she did not hesitate at committing any other crime, even the most dreadful, and she therefore made up her mind that she would kill the mother of Nang Hsen Gaw so that she could be the chief wife. She got home much sooner than the other woman, as she had no load to carry, and when she saw her husband he naturally asked her where the fish were. "Now," she thought, "here's a good chance to get that woman out of the way," so she told her husband that his other wife was a *pör*, or witch, and she had taken all the fish away from her. Now, witches are of course very much dreaded, so when the poor woman came home with her heavy load of fish, the villagers killed her with their sticks, and she was changed into a tortoise in the lake.

And now at last the mother of Nang E was chief wife, but do you think she was satisfied? Not a bit of it. She heard that her rival was now a tortoise in the lake, and she determined to kill her again.

Some time after this, as Nang Hsen Gaw was in the jungle watching the cows that belonged to her father, she walked along the edge of the lake and was very much surprised to hear her own name called in familiar tones. She looked around, but could see no one, and she was getting very frightened, thinking that it was perhaps a *hpea* who wanted to entice her into the thick jungle so that he could devour her, but at last she looked on the ground at her feet and saw it was a tortoise that was speaking to her.

"Nang Hsen Gaw," it called. "My daughter, *oie!* I am your mother who was killed through the wicked acts of my rival, the mother of Nang E. I have arrived at great trouble, and now, instead of being the chief wife of a rich man, I am nothing but a tortoise swimming in the lake. Take pity on me, my daughter, and out of compassion every day bring me cotton thread and raw cotton, so that I can weave and spin."

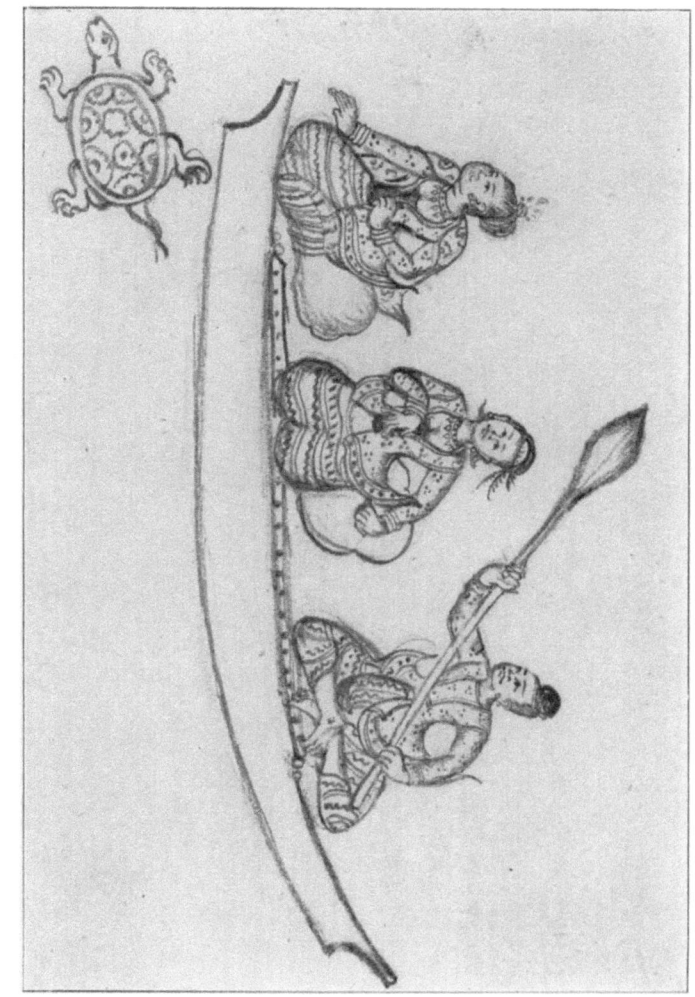

"I am nothing but a tortoise swimming in the lake."

Page 68.

Nang Hsen Gaw was a dutiful daughter, and every day when she went to the jungle she took cotton for her mother to spin, and thread for her to weave, and daily talked with her, telling her all the gossip of the village and anything else that she thought her mother would like to hear.

But the mother of Nang E was on the watch, and thinking it strange that the girl should take cotton and thread to the jungle every day, and bring none back with her when she drove the cattle back at night, she followed her, heard her talking with her mother, and thus found out in what part of the lake her enemy was, and laid her plan accordingly.

That evening, unknown to her family, while her husband was busy working in his garden, she went to the house where lived the doctor of the village, unfolded her plans to him and asked for his help. Being an unscrupulous man he agreed, took the silver the woman had pilfered from her husband, and promised to help her. The next day she was taken very sick and her husband called in the doctor, who told him that the woman must have a tortoise from the lake near-by. If she boiled and ate it according to his directions she would get well, if not, she would die. Having performed his part of the bargain he returned to his home at the other end of the village.

Next morning the man went to the lake to get the tortoise. Nang Hsen Gaw was much distressed when she saw her father set out, and her distress became worse when she saw that the wicked stepmother had directed him to the little pond where her own mother was. The man took a large bucket made out of wicker work, and commenced baling out the water, but Nang Hsen Gaw was able to warn her mother just where her father was, so that when he was on one side of the pond her mother went to the other, but at last he sent the girl home, and in a few minutes secured the tortoise and was soon carrying it away for his wife to eat.

When he got home he gave her the tortoise, little thinking who it was, and then went out, while the witch called Nang Hsen Gaw to watch the pot which had been put over the fire.

Soon the poor girl heard her mother call out. She said that the hot water had reached her knees, and begged her to put out the fire. She commenced to rake out the hot embers from under the pot, when her step-mother saw what she was doing, and taking up a heavy bamboo beat her unmercifully and made her put more sticks on the fire. Soon her mother complained again that the heat had reached her shoulders, and again Nang E's mother beat her, and made her put more sticks on the fire. Soon she heard her mother say: "My daughter, *oie!* The hot water has reached my neck and I shall soon be dead. When it is all over, do not let that wicked woman destroy me altogether, but bury me in the jungle," and in a few minutes she was dead.

Nang Hsen Gaw tried her best to get the dead body of her mother, but her stepmother watched her carefully, and all she could not eat herself she gave to the dogs, to prevent her daughter from getting any, but one dog ran off with his portion into the jungle. Nang Hsen Gaw followed in time to rescue the webbing between the fingers.[1] This was all that was left, but she buried that carefully in the jungle far from the house where her stepmother lived.

The next day as she was walking through the jungle feeding her cows, she heard sweet music. It sounded like twelve organs all playing at the same time, and yet in harmony, each organ blending with the others. In great surprise she hunted around till she came to the spot where she had buried the part of her mother's hand, and saw that during the night this had changed into a beautiful *mai nyung kham* tree.[2] And so this good and dutiful daughter went every day to listen to the tree as she had gone daily to the lake when her mother had been a tortoise, and the tree sang sweeter when she was near than at any other time.

But such a wonderful thing as this could not be kept a secret. Others heard of it and people came from far and near to hear the sweet music come from the tree. One of the *amats* of the great king who "ate"[3] the country, heard that a miracle was to be seen in this jungle, and accordingly reported it to his lord, who sent men to cut the tree down and bring it to his palace. All day long the men worked at the tree, from the time the

---

[1] The Shans call the two front feet of a quadruped "hands." The digits are called "fingers" not "toes."

[2] The sacred peepul tree.

[3] The Shans do not usually say that a king "rules" over a country, but the expression generally used is that he "eats" it; a very suggestive and alas! too often only too true expression.

country became light till the moon rose at night, but although they had the sharpest of axes and were the most skillful workmen in all the country, yet with all their labor they could only cut through the bark, and during the night the tree grew so quickly that when the morning dawned, it was twice as large as it was the night before, and the marks made by the axes on the bark were covered with new bark harder than ever.

The king was very angry when he heard of the ill success of his woodmen, had them all executed, and sent others, but they had no better success than the first. But this only made the king more stubborn and determined to get the tree at any cost, and he therefore sent the heralds all through the country and made a proclamation that any man who could bring the tree to his palace should be made his *Kem Möng*, that is, heir apparent; should it be a woman, she should become *Nang Me Prah*, or chief queen. Many men therefore came with sharp *pahs* and axes but all were equally unsuccessful, and the king despaired of ever getting the tree, when Nang Hsen Gaw heard of the reward offered by the king, and told the heralds she could bring the tree to his palace. The king was full of joy when he heard this, and made great preparations for her. On her part she simply went to the jungle and, taking off her turban, fastened it around the tree and carried it bodily into the palace where it sang as sweetly every day as when it was in the jungle.

When the mother of Nang E heard of the good fortune that had befallen Nang Hsen Gaw she was very

angry, and calling her own daughter to follow her, she
set off for the capital. When she had arrived there she
disguised herself and became a servant to the queen,
and pondered how she could kill the *Nang Me Prah* and
put her own daughter Nang E in her place.

One day this wicked woman told the queen that she
had found some fine soap beans and bark, that she was
very skillful in shampooing, and as the next day was to
be a great feast when the queen would follow the king
on her royal elephant, the soap beans would make her
black hair blacker, and the gloss glossier than ever,
and asked her to allow her to wash the queen's head at
a well that was just outside the gate of the palace, near
the royal gardens, where the water was very sweet.
The queen consented and called her attendants to follow, but the stepmother was much too cunning to allow
that, so she told the queen that her method of washing
was better than any other woman's but it was a secret,
and she would reserve it for her majesty's own private
use, but she did not want any of the attendants to see
how it was done. If they did, she added, the next day
at the feast every lady in the court would have hair as
glossy as the queen's, but if they went alone, her hair
would be as much more beautiful than any other
woman's as the sun is more beautiful than the bamboo
torch that lights the way through the jungle at night,
when there is no moon. The young queen was not
proof against this flattery, and so the two women went
alone out of the palace, the very guards who watched
at the gates not knowing whither they were going.

They soon arrived at the well, and as the queen was bending over, her long hair covering her face so that she could see nothing, her wicked stepmother suddenly drew a knife and stabbed her to the heart, then, calling her daughter to help, she buried the poor young queen under the road leading to the well. She took the royal robes and put them on her own daughter, Nang E, who returned to the royal palace and entered the royal apartments, all the attendants thinking it was the real queen returned from a bath in the river.

That same afternoon, as the king walked through the palace, he was surprised to see that the wonderful singing tree was all withered and mute. In great distress he called for the queen and ordered her to make the tree sing as before, but although Nang E tried with all her might, she could make no sound. She tapped it softly as she had seen Nang Hsen Gaw do, but all in vain. It was silent.

Now the king was in the habit of wearing Burmese clothing instead of Shan, and one day when he had gone to his room to put on his *ptsoe*, he found that a little sparrow had built, her nest in it. He was a very kind man, and so allowed the little bird to live there, and in gratitude to the king this sparrow was in the habit of telling him all she saw as she flew around the city from morn to night, and whenever the king wished to find out anything that puzzled him, he would often call the sparrow to tell him what to do.

He therefore now called the little bird and asked it what ailed the tree, and the sparrow told him that the woman who was then in the royal apartments and wearing the clothes of the *Nang Me Prah* was not the real queen, but a woman named Nang E, and seeing her approach, the brave little bird began whistling, "This is not the *Nang Me Prah*, this is Nang E, Nang E. Oh! Nang E!"

In a great rage the king commanded his servants to call the woman, and when she was come into the royal presence she dared not open her mouth to answer the king, for she was not so clever as her mother, who could disguise her voice as well as her face, and she knew that if she began to speak the king would see that she was not Nang Hsen Gaw, so she remained silent.   But this did not save her, for the king looked at her and said :

"You wear the robes and jewels of my queen, but you have not the same face, and you are afraid to speak to me," and he immediately called his chief executioner to take her away and cut off her head.

But even this did not bring back the music to the tree, and the king was disconsolate.

The next morning when the guard of the royal garden went to his post, he saw, near the well, a beautiful *mawk moo* flower, took it home with him and placed it in the *chattie* of water that every Shan keeps in his house as an offering to the *hpeas*. The old mother Nai, soon after took her basket and went to the bazaar to buy *puc* for her son's breakfast, but when she returned she was surprised to see that during her absence some one had swept the house, cooked the food, and that the

"morning rice" was all ready to eat. The eating-tray
was set out in the middle of the room. The rice and
curry was arranged in order on it, and the drinking
chattie was full of scented water. She called her son
and all the neighbors to ask who had done this, but no
one could tell her, and in great amazement they sat
down to their meal. That evening the same thing happened again. While she was out, the house was again
swept, the food was prepared, and the tray arranged
as in the morning. For several days this happened,
and then the old woman determined to hide and see
who did these kind acts. She did so, and was amazed
to see that as soon as she had left the house (she went
under the floor and looked up through a hole between
the bamboos), that a spirit came out of the *mawk moo*
flower that her son had brought from the road leading
to the well, and commenced to sweep the house. In the
midst of it the old woman rushed up to the flower and
destroyed it, so that the spirit could not go back to its
refuge. At the same instant, it changed into the most
beautiful woman ever seen.

That afternoon, Nang Hsen Gaw, for the spirit was
she, told old Nai how her stepmother had killed her
at the well, and buried her, and how she had been
changed into the spirit of the beautiful *mawk moo* flower
the guard had brought to the house, and that she would
soon go back to the king in the palace.

They neither of them had seen the little sparrow sitting on the roof, but she had been there all the time,
and now flew off to the king and told him all that she

had heard. The king gave orders that the wicked mother of Nang E should be executed immediately, and that a band of soldiers should go to the guard's house to escort his bride back in state to the palace, where she reigned many, many years, till she saw her grandchildren and great-grandchildren grow up. As soon as the queen entered the gate, the tree began to play; the withered leaves put on a bright hue, and beautiful flowers burst into bloom ; and while Nang Hsen Gaw lived, the tree bloomed and played sweetest music every day.

The lessons that this story teaches are : As surely as the wheels of the cart follow the oxen, so surely will wickedness be punished. If you sin you must suffer. The man who kills another will assuredly meet the same fate.

THE SPARROW'S WONDERFUL BROOD.

MANY, many years ago, at the beginning of the world, a little sparrow built her nest on the top of a tall tree that grew near the edge of a lake. In it she laid five little eggs, and never was mother bird prouder than she, and all day long she flew from tree to tree chirping out her joy. So proud in fact was she, and so much noise did she make, that a monkey that lived on the other side of the lake was struck with the remembrance of how he had once dined with great satisfaction on eggs laid by the sparrow's sister, and in a few minutes he was on his way to repeat the performance.

In vain the little bird cried and begged him to spare her brood, promising to show him where the sweetest plantains in all the country were growing; the monkey only laughed at her and climbed the tree to get the prize.

The next moment the robber would have gotten his spoil, and this wonderful story would never have been told, but just then the great lord Sa Kyah looked earthward and saw the tragedy that was taking place.

Like a drop of rain that falls from a tree when the wind blows after a shower, the mighty lord descended, and when the would-be robber reached the nest his hand entered an empty one.

"On his way he saw what seemed to be a bed of flowers."

Page 79.

The eggs were soon brought back from the *hpea* country where the lord Sa Kyah had taken them for safety, and in due time were hatched. Out of the first protruded a sharp bill, and a king-fisher, bright of plumage and swift of wing, broke out of its speckled prison. The next egg broke and a buffalo came out, to be followed by a lordly striped tiger from the next. A terrible *hpea-loo*, with head and claws like a bird and body like a man, tore his way out of the next one, already looking around for a man whom he might devour for his first meal.

Only one egg remained, and that the smallest of all, but out of it came a man, and the mighty lord Sa Kyah smiled when he saw him, and said that although he was the smallest and the last, yet he must feed his brothers and take care of them.

One hot day in summer the buffalo that had come out of one of the eggs, walking through the jungle, much troubled by mosquitoes, thought how nice would be a wallow in a hole well known to him under the shade of the trees by the bank of the lake, where the sun had not dried the mud to the hardness of bricks as it had in every other wallow, and accordingly turned his huge body in its direction, and slowly set off toward it.

On his way there he saw on the ground what appeared to him to be a bed of flowers growing on the bank of the lake, and after smelling it carefully over, leisurely ate it all up.

The sun was hot, the earth dry, and the flowers had long ago died, and what the buffalo thought were flowers were really ten white jackets and ten red skirts. But when he had finished his meal he continued his journey to the wallow, and then with a grunt expressive of great satisfaction, sinking into the soft mud till only the tips of his horns and the top of his head were visible, he closed his eyes and enjoyed himself.

By and by there was a great commotion in the water —shouts, laughter, and jokes, together with a great splashing. The lazy buffalo opened one eye and saw ten young girls who were having great fun in the cool water, throwing it over one another and chasing each other here and there. When they came to the place where they had left their clothes, however, their mirth received a sudden check. They had all disappeared ! They stood up to their armpits in the water looking at each other with very long faces till, spying the buffalo in his mud bath, they approached him, and in the most courteous language asked him whether he had seen their dresses.

The great beast closed the eye he had opened, and slowly uncovered the other one, but beyond this took no notice of the maids forlorn. Then, calling him "Kind Brother Buffalo," they begged him to answer them, saying that all the people who left the village to go to the bazaar before the sun had risen would soon be passing on their way home. The buffalo blew a big cloud of mud and water from his nostrils, but said never a word.

Now it happened that the youngest of the sparrow's brood, the man, was in the jungle all the time. He had seen his brother eat up all the clothes and had heard all the conversation. He had noticed too, that although all the maidens were beautiful, the youngest was the most beautiful girl he had ever seen. He saw how straight was her form, how black was her hair, and that her eyes were the color of the sky when there are many stars but no moon, and he determined to get her for his wife. He therefore now approached the party and told them that he could help them, and that no one besides could tell them where their clothes were, but that they must promise that the one whom he should pick out should be his wife.

To this they agreed, and thus it happened that he became possessed of the most beautiful woman in all the Shan country. So beautiful in fact was she, that it is said the birds stopped in the middle of a song when they saw her. The squirrels stopped half-way up the tree in their search for nuts as she walked under the trees, and her fame spread far and wide.

At this time a hunter came wandering through the jungle in search of game, and saw her standing at her door. He, like everybody else, was struck with her wonderful beauty, and he thought to himself, " For a long time I have been most unfortunate. I have caught but few animals, and their furs have been poor and mangy. Now, if I tell the king of my country about this beautiful girl, he will give me a great reward."

Thus reasoning he set out home and told the king what he had seen, enlarging upon her great beauty till the king resolved to get her at any cost.

F

He therefore set out, taking with him soldiers and attendants as became such a mighty lord, and when he saw the object of his journey he acknowledged that the hunter had not deceived him, and he determined to take her back with him to the palace ; but at the same time he made up his mind to go about it in a cunning way.

Now this king had a wonderful fighting cock of which he was very proud, and which had never been beaten. It had a beak of iron and spurs as sharp as the knives that come from Lai Hka, and a voice so loud and piercing that every morning when he crowed every other rooster in the city scurried away in fright at the challenge.

The king, therefore, said that he and the woman's husband should have a cock fight. He would wager his country against the other's wife. In great sorrow the man went out into the jungle to think over his misfortune, and while sitting on the ground in a most disconsolate manner he heard a little bird calling his name, and looking up he saw his brother, the kingfisher, perched above him.

"O brother, do not fear," said the bright little bird. "I do not forget that you are my brother and have guarded me long, and now I will surely help you in your trouble."

When the time came for the fight, therefore, and the king's fighting cock stood proudly up, suddenly down from a tree flew the kingfisher, pecked him with his long, sharp bill, and then flew away before he could so

much as turn his head.   Time and again this happened
till the king's challenger finally stretched himself dead
on the ground.

The fight ending in this way, however, did not suit
the selfish king a bit, and he therefore said it was not
a fair fight, and brought out a large, fierce dog.   This
dog was the terror of the State, but the king said that
it should fight any other dog that could be brought
against it for the same stakes as before.   The tiger
brother, however, was on the watch, and before the
dog could get near his opponent, a blow from his paw
ended his career.

Still the king persisted in his unjust course, and now
declared that the wager should be finally settled by a
fight between two buffaloes.   Now the buffalo brother
was ashamed of the way in which he had treated the
girls in the water, and had long wished for an opportunity to retrieve his honor, so that he now fought with
such bravery against the royal buffalo that he speedily
conquered it.

Then the king, seeing that he was beaten every time,
threw off all disguise and said plainly that he had come
to get the girl for his wife, had brought soldiers to help
him if necessary, and he would take her in spite of
losing the different battles, and in spite of her husband
or anybody else.

He stepped forward to take her, but he did not
know that one more brother yet remained to be heard
from, for out of the jungle with a dreadful yell came
rushing the *hpea-loo*, his beak open, his claws out-

stretched, and king, soldiers, and courtiers all disappeared down his ravenous maw.

The next month the fortunate man with his beautiful wife became king in the place of his enemy, and lived to be the oldest monarch in the whole of the Shan country.

HOW THE WORLD WAS CREATED.

IN the beginning of the world, many, many cycles ago, so long ago, in fact, that no man knows how long it was, there were no trees, no hills, no land, nothing but water. The wind blew the waters hither and thither, sometimes in great waves, sometimes in quiet ripples; the wind blew, the waves rolled, and that was all.

Now it happened that Gong Gow, the Great Spirit Spider, felt weary with carrying around her heavy burden of eggs wrapped up so carefully in their white covering fastened to her waist, therefore she said to herself:

"I would fain place my eggs in a safe place, but know of none where they can hatch themselves without danger," so she searched through the universe to find a suitable place, and at last she spied the water that is now the world, and in it began to spin her web.

Backward and forward, forward and backward, round and round, in and out she wove, till at last all was done, and full of content she left her eggs in their web prison nest and journeyed away.

The wind blew and drove the water hither and thither as aforetime, and soon little pieces of solid substance caught in the meshes of the web, and behold! as the time passed the solid substance became more

85

solid till it formed mud and separated itself from the water, and when the mud had dried, lo ! it was the earth.

So the eggs of the great Spirit Spider were safely locked up within the earth ; by and by they hatched, and breaking forth there appeared the first man, Boo Pau, and the first woman, Myeh Pau, from whom all the ancient people who belonged to the first race were descended.

Many, many years passed and people lived out their lives, till one day the great earth caught fire. It burned fiercer than anybody's imagination can conceive, and it destroyed everything. All the beautiful forests with their green coverings of moss and leaves, all the cities which the first race had builded were burned down, till by and by there was naught more for the fire to consume, and it was then the end of the hot season ; the time of wet came soon after, and the rain fell upon the burning earth in such torrents that the whole sky was covered with the steam.

Now it happened that in Möng Hpea, the far-away land where dwell the powerful spirits whom we call "hsangs," the smell of the steam ascended and ascended till all the spirits smelled the sweet scent, and said to themselves :

"Behold, there appears a sweet smell arising from below, what can it be?" and there was much marveling at what could cause such sweet-smelling incense as that then ascending.

And it also happened that in Möng Hpea were nine

spirits, five of them males and four females, and these being of more adventurous spirit than their fellows, determined to find out for themselves where the sweet perfume came from. So they set out on their travels downward. They descended faster and faster, and the faster they descended the sweeter became the smell, till at last they landed upon this world of ours, and bending down to the earth they tore great handfuls of it out and ate it with the greatest relish.

It was morning time when they descended, and they fed upon the fragrant earth all day till the sun set and the shades of evening began to surround them, then the eldest of the spirits looked around upon his fellows, and said :

"Brethren, oie ! it is time that we ascended to our own country," and as the rest assented they stood up to return, but alas ! they could not rise, they had eaten so much earth it had made them too heavy to soar, and from that day to the day they died none of them ever found their way back to the beautiful country of the Hsangs, but had to spend all their lives upon this earth of ours.

Thus we see that it is earthly desires that keep us from the spirit country. We see, or we hear, we smell or desire some earthly thing. We get our desires, but they keep us pinned down to the earth. We cannot go to the spirit country because of them.

When the spirits discovered that they could not return to the Hsang country they agreed that they would marry each other and take up their abode upon this earth of ours.   But here arose a difficulty ; there were five male hsangs but only four females !   There was chance of a great quarrel, but the strongest of them, his name was Hsin Kyan, thought within himself :

"I am stronger than any of my brothers and could easily defeat them and marry whom I will, but what merit would there be in that ? I will ask them whether they would be willing to make me king and each of them give me of their daughters when they are old enough, then in time I shall have wives and power as well." Thus we see it is the man who is willing to control his desires and wait who becomes great.

Hsin Kyan's brethren were very glad to make the agreement and thus it was that he became the ruler of them all.   When the daughters of the others were old enough, they brought them to the king, and from that day it has been the custom for men to offer their daughters to the king.

Now it happened that the universal lord, Sa Kyah, who rules over all spirits and men looked earthward and saw the new kingdom that was established ; he became jealous and determined to kill Hsin Kyan and take his kingdom away from him.   But Hsin Kyan was very subtle and cunning, so he tattooed himself with charms of such great strength that even the mighty lord Sa Kyah could not kill him.   For many years they fought.   Great mountains were thrown by each combatant at the other, but Hsin Kyan could not defeat the lord Sa Kyah, neither could the lord Sa Kyah kill Hsin Kyan.

Our great ancestor Hsin Kyan had seven daughters, whose names to this day are remembered among us as they have been given to the different days of the week, from Nang Ta Nang Nooie, the eldest, after whom we call the first day of the week Wan Ta Nang Nooie, to Nang Hsa Ne, the youngest, and when the mighty lord Sa Kyah found that he could not kill their father, he spoke to these daughters and told them he was searching for one whom he would make his chief queen, and that if one of them would kill his enemy, their father, and bring to him his head, he would choose that one to be his queen and make her joint ruler of the universe ; with him she should govern everything created.

But the charms tattooed upon Hsin Kyan were very potent. Water would not drown him ; fire would not burn him; rope would not strangle him; and he was invulnerable against thrust of spear and stroke of sword, and although all seven of his daughters tried to kill him yet they were not able to do so and six of them gave up the attempt in despair.

One day, however, the youngest, she whom we worship on the seventh day of the week and because she was the smallest call it Wan Hsa Nae, was walking in the jungle, and as she was passing under a tree she saw a bird sitting upon its topmost branch. Now this girl knew how clever birds are, and so she said to it :

"Brother Bird, oie ! can you tell me how I can kill my father ? "

Now although this daughter was the youngest, yet

she was more lovely than all her sisters, and the bird
was so pleased with her that he said :

"Nang Hsa Nae, you are so beautiful that I will
tell you the secret of your father's charm. Water cannot drown him, fire cannot burn him, neither can sword
or spear wound him, but there is one way in which he
may be killed. Take you, seven strands of a spider's
web and twist them into a cord, then with a piece of
white bamboo make a bow ; with this you will be able
to cut off the head of your father and take it to the
mighty lord Sa Kyah, and oh ! " continued the clever
bird, " when you are his queen, do not forget the good
turn I have done you, and the debt of gratitude you
owe me therefor."

Nang Hsa Nae was full of joy when she learned
the secret of her father's charm and she promised
the little bird that when she became queen of the
universe she would grant him any desire that he craved.

That night when everybody else was asleep, Nang
Hsa Nae crept to her father's side and with the bow
made of the seven twisted strands of a spider's web
killed him and cut off his head.

With great joy she carried it to the universal lord.
He was very glad to find that his enemy was at last
dead, but although he had given his word to her, yet
he would not marry Nang Hsa Nae, for, said he, she
has killed her father although I could not conquer him.
Were I to marry her, who will go surety for her that
she will not do the same to me? So the wicked daughter did not gain her ambitious end after all.

Not only that, however, but she and her sisters received a punishment, one they are even now suffering, and will continue till the world ends. It is this :

When they found that the lord Sa Kyah would not marry their youngest sister or even accept their father's head, they said among themselves :

"What shall we do with the head of our father? Where shall we bury it? Should we place it in the earth the whole world would catch on fire ; should we throw it into the sea, all the seven oceans would immediately boil ; what shall we do ? "

In their distress they went to the mighty lord Sa Kyah and in humble tones begged his lordship to give them advice so that they would be freed from the terrible trouble to which their wickedness had brought them. He looked at them and said :

"This is what you must do. You," pointing to the youngest, "must carry your father's head in your arms all this year, and when the year is finished you can give it to the sister who is next older than yourself. She will carry it for a year and thus one of you will ever after bear it."

And so it is. We know when the year ends because then come the Wan Kyap or washing days, when the princess who has carried her father's head for a year gives it to her elder sister and washes the bloodstains from her clothes.

From these spirits all the inhabitants of the world are descended, and so we see the saying of our philosophers is true, "We have all descended from spirits."

HOW THE KING OF PAGAN CAUGHT THE THIEF.

MANY, many years ago there lived near the old city of Pagan a famous robber chief who was so fierce and cruel that he made all men fear his name. He stole and killed and burned till the mothers used to frighten their disobedient children by saying, "Boh Lek Byah will get thee." He was a very brave and clever thief, and he became so strong that the headmen and elders of all the towns and villages throughout the country were obliged to fee him with money and goods, and if by any chance they did not pay this blackmail immediately it was demanded, that very night the followers of the robber chief would assuredly burn down their village and kill every man, woman, and child within it, for this was Shan and Burmese custom.

Boh Lek Byah entered every house in Pagan. None was too big, none too small. He stole from the *whon's* house as easily as from the hut of the poor man ; it made no difference to him, till at last the palace where the great king lived was the only place whence he had not gotten booty. Several of his followers were caught and crucified, but that did not stop his bad actions or frighten him. In the old days, when a robber was caught he was taken to the jungle where the tigers are. All the tigers knew the place of execution as well as a

dog knows worship days when the women offer rice and
curry at the pagodas.   They used to tie the thieves fast
to the cross by their feet, hands, and hair, and when
they had jeered at them and the women and children
had pelted them with stones and beaten them with bamboos, everybody went home and left them for the tigers
to eat, and thus they did to the followers of Maung
Lek Byah, but they could never catch the robber chief
himself.

At last the people of Pagan city came to the Amat
Löng, who was next in rank to the king himself, and
said :

"Our lord, for long thy slaves have been in great
and sore trouble, and unless our lord takes pity upon
his servants we shall all arrive at destruction."

"What can I do?" cried the *amat*, in a loud, angry
voice, "has he not stolen from me ?   Did I not pay
him two whole *ticcals* of pure silver as protection money
no later than the last Water Feast, and yet did he not
rob me as I was coming home in my boat yesternight,
and when I told him that I was the Amat Löng, did
he not laugh in my face and yet rob me just the same.
What can I do?"

"Our lord can go to the Ruler of the Golden Palace
and plead for his slaves," suggested one of the suppli-
ants.

Now, the Amat Löng was a very cunning man, and
he knew that if the king heard that Boh Lek Byah
had stolen so much from his subjects he would be very
angry, and might perhaps even deprive him of his rank

as chief amat, for it was his duty to see that all robbers were caught and punished, therefore after thinking for a while, he said :

"My friends, listen to me; let us each give silver, as much as we can afford ; it is better to give part of our possessions than to have everything taken from us. Dost hear ? This silver we will give to the *boh*, and he will then not trouble us any more, but will go to towns where the people are poorer and cannot afford to give as much as we, the citizens of this royal city of Pagan; then shall we have peace."

This advice was very good and would have been acted upon, but unfortunately, one of the little princes happened to be in the audience chamber that morning and heard what had been said. He went to his father, the ruler of the Golden Palace, and told the king what he had heard; therefore his majesty called the *amat* to the Golden Foot and asked him of these things.

"What is this I hear ?" he demanded. "Has this wicked man robbed as much as the people say? Why hast thou not caught him as it was thy duty to do?"

"Son of the Sun," replied the servant, trembling very much as he kneeled before him, for who would not be afraid when the king is angry? "it is true; but this thief is a very wicked and clever thief, besides which he has a wonderful charm tattooed upon his body which is so potent that it makes him invulnerable to wounds from sword or gun, neither can he be bound with ropes, therefore it hath been impossible for the slave of our lord the king to capture or harm him."

"Then," said the king, still very angry, " get thee a charm still more potent than the one the robber chief hath, for if thou dost not bring him or his head to me ere three days have elapsed, thou shalt fall from thy rank of chief *amat*. Dost thou hear?"

The *amat* bowed till his head touched the floor before the Golden Foot and he crawled away from the presence the most unhappy man in all the king's possessions. Then in great haste he ran to his house and called all the charm-makers in the city to come to him without delay. Then when they had assembled before him he commanded them to make him a charm which would be stronger than the one tattooed upon the body of the robber chief, Boh Lek Byah. But the charm-sellers one and all declared that this was an impossibility, for the thief had upon the luckiest day of the whole year eaten a piece of flesh cut from the body of a murdered man, and so he could not be harmed in any way, neither was it in their power to give his lordship the amat a charm stronger than his.

Very frightened was the amat when he heard this, and very frightened were the soldiers who had been ordered to go with him and catch the thief. Their wives also cried all that night, for they knew what a terrible man the robber was, and how angry he would be with the men who had dared come to capture him. He would show no mercy, and without doubt would kill them all, and in derision send their heads back to the city afterward. This the robber had done before more than once to parties of soldiers sent to take him.

Now it happened that among the soldiers who followed the Amat Löng was one who had a very wise and clever wife, and when she saw her husband march away and knew the great danger that he and his fellows were in, she went to the wife of another soldier, and this is what she said :

"Sister, oie, listen to my words. If we do naught but sit in our houses and weep our husbands will all assuredly arrive at destruction, for the *boh* is a very cruel and cunning man. Of what use will our houses be to us if we have no husbands? Listen, therefore, to what I say. The man who collects the blackmail for the *boh* from the headman of a village across the river and delivers it into his hand is well known to me. His name is Maung Gyei, and he sells books in the bazaar. He is a very wise man, and knows all the followers of the Boh Lek Byah. Let our husbands fight the *boh* with silver. It is sharper than a sword, and injures not the man who handles it skillfully. We will collect all the money we can. I will sell my earrings, thou canst sell thy bracelets, and the wives of all the other soldiers can do likewise. This will bring a big bag of silver, and half of it we will give to Maung Gyei. He will then call some of the followers of the *boh* to a secret place and tell him that the Amat Löng will give him the balance in return for the head of their master, if they take it to his lordship ere three days have have elapsed. Our husbands will then bring the head of this wicked man to the royal palace and lay it before the Golden Foot ; they will reap much honor and glory for having fulfilled the order of the king and the country will be freed from this great trouble.

Now, when the wives of the other soldiers heard these words they perceived that she was indeed a very clever woman, fit to be the wife of a great *amat* instead of a common soldier, and one ran swiftly after the *amat* and his men, for in truth they had not gone far, but were traveling slowly, because they feared to come up with the *boh* and his fierce followers ; and they were filled with joy at the good news the messenger brought them.   At the order of the *amat* his men hid themselves in a thick jungle till the money should be collected and brought to them.

After two days and when it was very dark, a man came to them saying that he was the friend of Maung Gyei, and bore with him the head of the robber chief, and thereupon showed it wrapped up in a cloth.   Then were the soldiers full of joy again, and they paid the money to him, and that night they slept peacefully, for they knew that their enemy could harm them no more, and that they had been delivered from the great danger which had been threatening them.   Before they slept the *amat* sent a swift messenger to the city to tell the king the good news that the robber chief was dead, and that they were bearing his head with them and would present it before the Golden Foot the next morning.

Next day, therefore, at the head of his men, he marched to the Golden Palace, and the people of the city were so full of joy over the fact that Boh Lek

G

Byah was dead, that great numbers followed the procession to the palace gates in the hopes of getting a glimpse at the head of their enemy, and everybody praised the Amat Löng for his bravery and wisdom in killing the robber chief who had oppressed them so sorely.　His wife also called musicians and dancers, and gave orders to her servants to prepare a great feast that night in honor of her brave husband.　They reached the Golden Foot and knelt before the throne, but when the basket was opened, behold, it contained the head of another man, and not that of the *boh* at all.

Then did all the people in the city laugh at the *amat* because his enemy had deceived him, and he fell from his rank of chief *amat*.　All his golden umbrellas were taken away from him and given to his successor, and he was obliged to earn his living by selling medicines in bazaar, and from that day till he died he bore the nickname of Amat Toak Arah ;[1] but the people all praised the cleverness of his enemy, the thief.

Now, when the king saw how cunning Boh Lek Byah was and how easily he had deceived his servant, he determined that he himself would take the robber chief and thus gain great credit and renown.　To this end he gave orders to the headman of every village throughout his kingdom that directly the robber should come within his jurisdiction he was to report immediately, and the king would send a trusty officer to arrest him.　He did not tell them that he himself would go,

---

[1] Literally, "The counselor who fell from his rank," *i. e.*, was degraded.

therefore for a long time the headmen feared to obey
the order of the king for, said they among themselves:
" The *boh* deceived the Amat Löng, who was one of the
most cunning of men, and will he not escape from any
other whom it should please our lord the king to send
against him ? Is there any more cunning man in the
palace now than before ? When he finds out also that
we have reported his presence to the king his mind will
become hot against us, and he will without doubt return and destroy all our houses and kill everybody in
our village. Nay, it is better to give him silver and
beg him begone elsewhere," so although they told the
messengers of the king they would follow his words,
they simply held their peace when the dreaded robber
chief was near their village.

But after a long time the headman of Myo Haung,
who was braver than his fellows, came to the palace
and told the king that the *boh* was then at his village,
and would leave when it became dark, taking boat for
Myo Kywe, which was a suburb of the city of Pagan.

The heart of the king was filled with joy when he
heard this piece of good news, and he gave the headman
a great reward. Also he took off the royal robes such
as is the custom of kings to wear, and put on very poor
ones so that no one would think that he was the lord
who ate the country of Pagan. He also took with him
a sword ; not the royal sword with the silver sheath
and ivory handle, but an old dah with a wooden handle
bound around with rattan string, and a sheath of wood,
such as the common people carry, then he went to the

bank of the river near Myo Kywe and waited. He waited long, but his heart was strong and he did not become discouraged by reason of the waiting, and at last he saw coming down the river a small boat, and in it a man whom he knew immediately to be the thief.

Maung Lek Byah guided his boat toward the bank near where the king was seated, for he was a skillful oarsman, and when he had fastened it with a rattan loop to the end of his oar stuck into the soft mud at the water's edge he ascended the path to the village, and as he reached the top of the bank he caught sight of the king in his dingy clothes and wearing the old sword with the wooden handle, sitting on the side of the path.

He was surprised to see a man there at that time of night, for the gongs which call the priests and old women to worship had sounded long before, and everybody in the village was sound asleep, therefore he gazed earnestly at the king and then called out :

" Who is that ? "

" It is a man who wishes to arrive at the rank of disciple to our lord," replied the king.

" Art thou a man of the day or a man of the night ? " asked the robber looking down at him.

" Thy servant is a man of the night," replied the king.

" Hast thou not heard how many of my followers have been caught and executed ? How that the tigers at the entering in of the villages will not now eat oxen but wait till one of my men is tied up for them ? I

tell thee they have not long to wait either. Art thou
not afraid ? ''

"Ah, our lord," replied the king, "thy disciples
suffered because they did not take heed and follow in
the footsteps of our lord, therefore have they arrived
at destruction ; but thy servant will study thee, O
payah, and thus will I learn how to become a great
boh and also to escape their fate.''

Now when the king talked in this fashion the *boh*
was very pleased with him, and gave him permission to follow. He also promised to teach his new disciple all his arts ; that he would not let him ever be
caught and would make him as famous a *boh* even as
he was. "And so," said he, "as thou hast a sword
with thee, follow me. I will give thee thy first lesson.''

Now it happened that as they walked along toward
the city the thief began to think within himself, "Who
can this new disciple be? He surely comes from a
high family, for he speaks not like the common people,
but as kings have a custom of speaking. He wears the
clothes of a common man, and carries the sword of a
coolie, but yet his words are the words of one used to
command. Can he be a spy sent by the *amat* whom I
tricked so nicely the other day, I wonder?'' and thus
he turned it over and over in his mind.

The *hpeas* have ever aided the kings of Burma, and
now those whom the king had been in the habit of
feeding daily were watching over him, and when they
heard the *boh* thus talk with himself, for the spirits
can hear us think even when we make no sounds of

words, they put it into the head of the robber to go to
the house of the king's own astrologer. It was not
very far and they soon arrived there. Then Maung
Lek Byah said to the king :

"Stay thou here and watch ; if thou dost see or hear
aught come and call me," but he himself went under
the house of the astrologer to discover whether he slept
or not. When he knew that the man was sound asleep
he would draw a sharp knife which he carried in his
girdle, cut a hole in the mat side of the house, creep
in through this hole and take what he wished ; then he
would escape before the lord of the house awoke.

As he was watching, however, he heard the astrologer
come out upon the veranda so that he could study the
stars, for that was his custom ; then he heard him say
to himself :

"Truly this is a good thing to marvel at, for I see
the star of that famous robber chief, Boh Lek Byah,
and following it closely is the star of none other than
the ruler of the Golden Palace himself."

For a long time the astrologer sat upon his veranda
pondering over this strange occurrence and trying to
think what it should portend; but in vain. He could
think of no solution of the mystery, so after again saying
that it was a good thing to marvel at he gave it up and
went into his house to sleep.

Thus did the thief discover the high rank of his new
disciple, for the astrologer knew the star of the *boh* well
and would make no mistake. He also knew the star
of the king. Had this same astrologer not cast the

horoscope of the robber chief and foretold which days
were lucky and which unlucky to him, so that by taking heed he had never been caught?   Therefore when
he again came forth from under the royal astrologer's
house and saw the king was still waiting without, even as
he had given orders, his mind was filled with great fear.

Then said the king directly he saw the robber: " O
Kin Byah, thy servant knows a place where there are so
many rubies that they are as common as *maknin* seeds
that the children play with in the dust; gold is as
plentiful as iron is with us, and there is enough silk to
stock ten bazaars.   All this is within reach of our
hands.   I can guide thee to the place, for I know it
well ; wilt thou follow?"

Then said the thief: "I know of but one place of
which thou canst say that with truth, and that is the
Golden Palace; but a man may not enter there and
live.   Knowest thou not that the guards carry sharp
dahs, and that if a man is caught there without permission from the king or one of his *amats*, he is immediately impaled?   In very truth it is a place good to
shun and fear greatly, even as the den of a hungry
tiger in the jungle."

" True, O brave man," replied the king, " but this
evening as I passed by the palace I saw hanging from
the top of the wall a rope-ladder ; we can climb over,
take enough to make us rich for the rest of our lives,
and run away before the guards with the sharp *dahs*
discover that we have been there.   Thus shall we earn
much wealth and glory, and people throughout the

land will call our lord the 'Boh Who Entered the
Golden Palace,' and all men will fear his name more
than the name of a hungry leopard."

Then were the thoughts of the *boh* in great confu-
sion, and he said to himself: "Of a truth I am about
to arrive at destruction at last. I have had my last
adventure. If I do not follow the king he will assuredly call out to the guard and I shall be taken. If
I go, how shall I be delivered from the great dangers
which will surround me in the Golden Palace? I am
undone whichever way I take."

Then said he to the king: "O disciple, whom I love
much, I fear to enter the Golden Palace, for this I perceive is one of my unlucky days. We will therefore
go to Pin Tha village, for I saw this morning a great
number of coolies there. They were following a great
prince from the hills. They have been traveling far to-
day and are therefore heavy with sleep, and we can
despoil them of as much as we can carry away. As
they are very weary with their journey, none will know
aught till they awake in the morning."

"Upon what day wast thou born?" demanded the
king, and the *boh* said that it was upon a Saturday.

"Then," said the king, "behold! this is a lucky
day," and he drew forth from under his jacket a horoscope, which showed that this was a lucky day upon
which a man who had been born upon a Saturday
could undertake any deed requiring great wisdom and
bravery in its accomplishment, and in spite of all that
Maung Lek Byah could say the king led the way

toward the palace, and the *boh* was obliged to follow him, which he did with very slow and hesitating steps, for his heart had become as weak as water.

Even as the king had said, there was a rope-ladder hanging over the palace wall, and the *boh* perceived in what manner the king had left the Golden Palace, but being a very wise man he followed without opening his mouth.

They passed through the palace courtyard and saw there a thing good to marvel at ; all the guards who ought to have been watching their lord were slumbering, so that the king and the *boh* gathered up all the spears and *dahs* belonging to these men and carried them away, hiding them in a secret place under one of the houses.

As they entered the palace buildings the thief became so full of alarm that all his strength left him and he could hardly walk. Then the king saw that his follower had arrived at great fear, and as they passed the house where the royal food was prepared, he said :

"Friend, I perceive that thou art in sore distress ; come, eat the food I am about to prepare for thee and thou wilt become strong."

"Nay," said the *boh*, "that I cannot do. Can a common man eat of the golden food and live? This will I not do; surely I should be accounted worthy of death." The king would not listen to him, but entered the royal kitchen, and with his own hands cooked some food which he compelled the thief to eat.

Now, the king had prepared two messes, one in

which he had cunningly placed some opium and one
without, and it was the food which contained the opium
that the king gave to the *boh*.   Therefore, after a little
time, he said to the king :

"O disciple of mine, I know not what is the matter
with me.   I have no strength and although it is death
to sleep in the Golden Palace yet must I sleep, for if I
do not I shall surely die."

As he said these words his head drooped upon his
chest, his eyes closed and he fell asleep.   Once more
was the heart of the king filled with joy and he bound
the *boh* with strong ropes in great haste and made him
a prisoner.

Early the next morning the king called the officer
who was in charge of the guard the night before and
when he was come before the face of his majesty, the
king said :

"I have a parable to tell thee.   Once upon a time
there was a great king and in his country was also a
famous robber chief and, behold, one night the king
was sore troubled with questions of statecraft so that he
could not sleep, therefore he walked throughout his
palace.   As he was passing through the courtyard he
spied a ladder hanging from the top of the wall.   Now
the thief of whom I have spoken had that very night
entered the Golden Palace and at that same moment
the king caught sight of him, loaded down with plun-
der, creeping toward the rope ladder beside which he
stood.   Then the king fell upon him and took him
prisoner, bound him securely with strong ropes and

dragged him to a safe place ; but the soldiers who should
have been watching were all asleep.   What should be
done to such guards as these ? ''

Now the officer did not yet know that the *dahs* of his
men had been stolen, so bowing before the Golden Foot,
he replied :

" Head of thy servant's body, there is but one thing
to be done, they are worthy of death.   Their lord should
pass judgment upon them without mercy and that immediately.''

" That is a good judgment,'' replied the king, and
turning again to the officer of the guard, he said :

" Last night I saw the great and renowned robber
chief, Boh Lek Byah, in this palace.   I took him prisoner with mine own hands, behold, he lies tied fast
with ropes in yonder room, but all the guards who
should have been watching were asleep.   Where are
their *dahs ?*   Let every man who has no sword be impaled before I eat my morning rice.''

Then were the hearts of the king's *amats* full of joy
when they heard that the thief whom they all feared
was a prisoner in the palace, and they praised the won-
drous bravery and subtlety of their royal master, saying that without doubt he was the bravest and wisest
king who ever sat under a white umbrella.

The king was very proud as he listened to their
praises and gave orders that the robber chief should be
brought before him.

When Boh Lek Byah was led to the Golden Foot he
prostrated himself, and the king said :

" If a man be found in the royal palace at night what hath custom decreed should be the punishment for his presumption ? "

Then the prisoner said: " King above all kings, it is death."

" Hast thou anything to say why thou shouldst not be impaled or given to the tigers to eat ? " demanded the king in a terrible voice.

" Lord of the world," replied the unfortunate man, " last night thou didst ask to become disciple to our lord's slave. Will the disciple order his teacher to be executed ? When our lord's slave was beneath the royal astrologer's house he discovered that his new disciple was the Eater of the Country and so when our lord of the Golden Palace ordered his slave to enter, he would have been worthy of death had he not obeyed. Will the Son of the Sun execute his slave for following his words ? "

Then when the king heard that the robber had known who he really was, he marveled much at his wisdom, and said :

" Assuredly thou art too wise a man for the tigers to eat. Take thou yonder sword, it belonged to him who yesterday was captain of the royal guard. Follow me and thou shalt later become my chief *amat*."

GLOSSARY OF TERMS

Puc. Curry.

Zayat. A place built for the accommodation of travelers, also used as an assembly place for worship, especially during religious feasts; they are usually built near monasteries.

Parah. (Burmese, *payah*) a god; an image of Gautama Buddha.

Kam. Luck.

Mau. To be skillful.

Amat löng. The chief amat or chief counselor of a prince.

Soie. The Indian "*viss*"; a weight equal to about three and a half pounds avoirdupois.

Chattie. A cooking pot, usually made of earthenware.

Hük. A deep rent in the earth with steep sides; a ravine; a torrent usually runs in it during the rainy season, but it is dry in the hot season.

Hpea. Spirit or supernatural being.

Amat. A minister of State.

Hsan. A rice bag.

Nang Me Prah. A queen.

www.ingramcontent.com/pod-product-compliance
Lightning Source LLC
Chambersburg PA
CBHW020151180626
46810CB00004B/1848